WHICH SISTER

WHICH SISTER

A PSYCHOLOGICAL THRILLER

JACK DANE

ALSO BY JACK DANE

Both had a reason...but which sister killed him?

Judith, the younger Rose sister, has always been more successful. After marrying Mark, her sister Katie's former husband, she finally has it all. The perfect job, apartment, and relationship. The **perfect** life...until **secrets** about Mark come to light. **Secrets worth killing over**.

Katie couldn't be a more total opposite. After her alcoholism ended her marriage, her life began to spiral. And when Mark seeks full custody of their young daughter, Katie has **nothing left to lose**.

So when Mark goes missing in Central Park, all eyes turn to the Rose sisters. Both have a reason to kill Mark— and **both have something to hide**.

As the police begin to dig into the sisters and their **bitter feud**, two facts become clear: Someone is **guilty**, and **no one can be trusted**.

Only one question remains...which sister is a killer?

PROLOGUE

EMAIL DRAFT, 5:04 PM

My name is Mark Wharton. If you're reading this, then that means I'm already dead.

Someone is out there. I can hear them. I think they're coming for me.

I know I haven't lived a perfect life. I don't think any of us have. I've made my fair share of mistakes.

*But right now, I can only think of two people who would kill me over those mistakes. If I'm dead, then it was by the hand of one of the **Rose sisters**.*

I'm hiding right now, but if

PART 1

ONE
KATIE

I jerk upright with a grunt.

Blinking hard, I hold still to listen. *Knock-knock-knock.*

That *was* a knock I heard, it wasn't just imagined. My eyes slide to the alarm clock on the table beside my disheveled bed.

As soon as the time registers in my sluggish brain, my stomach drops.

Oh no.

My face flushes with heat as I launch myself out from underneath the covers, head whipping about frantically as I try and locate a pair of pants. The knocking is louder now, more insistent.

"Coming," I shout, my voice a little hoarse as it carries through the apartment.

I hear the other bedroom door creak open. Amelia's going to answer the knocking herself.

Not a good look for me.

"Mommy will get it," I shout in the direction of my door.

I've snatched up a loose pair of sweatpants and work them up around my waist as I shuffle to my bedroom door. I wrench it open, but only halfway as a shirt on the floor stops the door's progress.

Through the gap, I see Amelia reach up and open the front door while I can do nothing but watch helplessly.

"Hello Daddy," she says in her sweet five-year-old voice, her excitement palpable.

"Hello sweetheart," I hear Mark say.

I can only make out his shoulder from this angle. Ducking down, I yank the shirt out from underneath the door. With the obstacle removed, I'm finally able to get out of the bedroom and hustle toward Amelia and Mark, his full body coming into view in the doorway.

His eyes move from our daughter up to me, and the disappointment that overtakes his face is immediate.

My cheeks flush again as I reach the door, working hard to restrain my chest from rising and falling.

"Hey. Sorry," I say, more than a little breathless from the exertion and the panic of oversleeping.

Ignoring me, Mark puts his hand atop Amelia's little head. "Why don't you go gather your things sweetheart."

Amelia races off, leaving me alone in the doorway with her father. As soon as Amelia is out of earshot, Mark's eyes slide back to my face.

"Is everything okay?" he asks in a measured voice.

He's trying to sound casual, like he's not interrogating me, but I read through it.

He thinks I drank again last night. I can just tell from his expression.

Running a hand through my frazzled hair, I straighten my spine a little. "All good. My shift ran late last night, that's all."

Mark studies me for another moment before finally nodding. "Okay," he says.

The sound of footsteps in the hallway draws my gaze to one of my neighbors walking by. Our eyes meet for a moment as she glances between Mark and me. It makes me even more conscious of the vast difference in appearance between me and my ex-husband.

Where Mark's dress shirt is crisply ironed, his hair perfectly parted, I'm wearing a loose t-shirt with a stain and the aforementioned baggy sweatpants.

I can't imagine what's going through the mind of the woman walking by. She's probably wondering how a man like Mark ever got mixed up with a woman like me.

My gut twists a little as I hike up the sweatpants.

Amelia reappears, her pink-sparkle backpack slung over her shoulder. It's packed to the brim with her clothes, toys and toiletries. My heart pangs as I catch sight of the excitement written plainly across her face at the prospect of leaving.

Mark's expression transforms into a smile as Amelia comes up to us.

"All packed up?" he asks, to which Amelia nods.

"Got everything," she says.

"Toothbrush?" Mark asks.

"Dad, I said I got everything."

Mark winks at her. "Just making sure. Okay, say goodbye to Mommy."

Amelia turns back to me, the keychains hanging off her backpack jingling.

"Goodbye Mommy," she says.

I squat down in front of her so that our eyes are level.

"Goodbye, baby. I love you, I love you so much," I say, searching her eyes as I say it.

Amelia looks away, slightly uncomfortable as I pull her little body into a hug. I squeeze her tight with my eyes shut, knowing I won't be able to see her until next weekend.

As we part, my eyes are a little misty, but I do my best to cover it up for her sake.

"Okay, bye," Amelia says, giving me a wave as she reaches up for Mark's hand.

"See you next weekend," he says to me as he directs Amelia out the door.

I nod hurriedly, biting my lip as I watch the two of them start down the hallway together away from my door. Amelia bounces with each step as she walks, her neck craned up to look at her father.

Seeing her adoring expression makes my chest ache even more. She doesn't look at me like that. Not anymore.

Not after everything I've done.

My mind drifts back to the expression of pure disappointment on Mark's face when he saw me stumbling out of the bedroom. I knew exactly what he was thinking at that moment, and it hurt.

I suppose there's no one but myself to blame for that.

That's what Dad would say, if he were still alive. His no-nonsense business talk didn't just stay in the boardroom.

But I was telling the truth. I didn't drink last night after work. It's not like I have no control over myself or something. Obviously, he suspected otherwise.

I've seen that look too many times before, and that's probably why it stung. It was there on his face when I woke up in the hospital, and later when he told me he wanted a divorce.

If I could remember any of his wedding to my sister, I'm sure I would've seen the look again.

Crashing that event completely drunk probably didn't help my case. But still... my *sister*.

My own sister stole my husband.

At this point, I don't know which one I'm more angry with—her or him.

TWO
MARK

Holding Amelia's hand, I lead her down the hallway toward the stairwell.

It's stained and dingy, like the rest of this apartment building. Patches of paint are missing from places across the ceiling.

I don't exactly love Amelia spending her time in a place like this every weekend, but it's all Katie can afford on her pay. Her share of her inheritance has long since vanished, despite it being quite sizable to start. Addiction really is a black hole.

"How was your weekend?" I ask as Amelia and I start down the stairs.

She nods, taking the stairs two at a time as she leaps down them. "Good."

"Do anything fun with Mommy?" I ask.

Amelia tilts her head and pauses for a moment to think before shaking no.

"Not really. Mommy had work, so I just watched a lot of Scooby-Doo with Nora. That part was fun."

I nod, biting my lip as we reach the first-floor landing. Nora is the teenage daughter of one of the other people in the building who Katie pays to babysit.

There's another question I want to ask, though I'm not sure I really want to hear the answer.

"Watch that puddle," I say with a wag of my chin toward the shiny spot on the tile floor in the building's entryway.

Amelia skirts around it. I push open the front door, and we're greeted with a refreshing wall of cool fall air.

"Race you to the car," I say. Amelia grins and lets out a squeal as she takes off.

I've got the car double-parked a few spots up the street, so time is of the essence. My daughter reaches the car first, turning around to gloat as the wind blows trash and dried leaves toward us.

A gust of it ruffles my hair, and instinctually I stop to peer into the window of the car parked beside me to reset it. Judith hates to see a hair out of place.

"I won, Daddy," Amelia says as I come up to the car, key fob in hand.

"Yes you did. Total blowout," I say as the car doors click unlocked.

"Does this mean I don't have to go to school today?"

Chuckling, I help her up into the backseat and strap her into her booster seat. "Not quite, young lady. Nice try."

Once we're loaded up and buckled in, I glance once more at Katie's apartment building. The brick facade looms overhead, casting shadows onto the street that cut into the early morning light. I'm reminded again of those dark days when we first separated, and she moved in here.

I haven't thought about those days in a while. Katie has been doing really well since then, though today was a slight departure from that.

Maybe she really was telling the truth, and she just overslept today.

Then again, Katie is an alcoholic.

I'm not sure I can really trust anything she says, as much as I want to. And I can't forget that she endangered our child.

With a small sigh, I ease the car into drive and get us moving toward Amelia's school.

The Bordley School is the kind of private school I would've ridiculed growing up.

Back then, I couldn't ever have imagined I'd be one of those people sending my five year old to a Kindergarten that costs over sixty thousand dollars a year. Even once I started making real money, I wasn't completely sold on the idea.

Judith however, insisted on it. Part of me wonders if her insistence was really entirely about Amelia's education, or if Judith just wanted to erase Katie's influence as thoroughly as possible.

In any case, I've learned arguing with Judith is impossible. She isn't her sister—in fact, they're complete opposites.

Initially, that was a point of attraction for me. The total juxtaposition of personalities.

When Katie was at her worst, Judith's unrelenting strength and stoicism helped keep me afloat.

Compared to the disaster that was my personal life at the time, Judith was like a sparkling diamond atop a pile of rubble. Attractive, supportive, smart. Ready and willing to help with whatever I needed.

It wasn't until we were married that I truly understood how Judith was able to be so perfect.

Every. Single. Thing. Is. Regimented.

Her maiden name should've been Rules, not Rose. Always more rules.

I understand that her father was some mega-successful business exec here in the city, and that's part of the reason she's so driven. Success was mandatory. Judith and Katie responded to that demand in opposite ways, that's for sure.

"Daddy, it's green."

Blinking, I look up at the light and realize Amelia's right. Pressing down on the gas, I pass through the intersection and then begin looking for the Holy Grail, an open parking spot near the school during morning drop off time.

The Bordley School towers above us, its ornate stone exterior a testament to its grandeur.

By some miracle I find a spot across the street just a few spaces down from the entrance and pull over before putting the car in park. Amelia removes her seatbelt and shifts across the back seat to the other side.

She opens her door, her black, buckled dress shoes hitting the sidewalk as I unbuckle myself and slide out.

The early morning air is filled with the sounds of school-day hustle and bustle, car doors opening and shutting, parents wishing their children a good day, kids chattering and laughing as they greet each other. In the distance, a siren wails as I close my door.

Rounding the car, I grab hold of Amelia's hand, and together we wait until a couple cars roll by and then cross the street.

Other children approach the school as well, some coming out of the backs of long black cars driven by chauffeurs in black suits.

We aren't quite at that level of wealth yet, and I'm not sure I'd like to be. Taking Amelia to school is one of my favorite things to do in the world, even if it means having to wake up at the literal crack of dawn.

These aren't times I'll be able to get back though, so it's worth it. Amelia tugs a little at my arm, wanting us to move faster once she sees one of her friends.

As I look up at the school's open doors, I spot someone too.

Our eyes meet for a moment, and then I look away, feeling my heart beat a little faster.

Now that we've safely crossed the street, I squat down on the sidewalk and give Amelia a once over.

"Have a great day and learn lots, okay?" I say, brushing a spot of lint off the shoulder of her uniform sweater.

Amelia nods hurriedly, hugging me quickly and exchanging "love you's" before rushing off to greet her friend. I watch her go, a small smile on my face as the wind blows and lifts her hair, making it dance around her head.

"Mr. Wharton."

I turn to see Mia—I mean Ms. Goodridge—standing just beside me. Amelia's kindergarten teacher.

She's wearing a pencil skirt that hugs closely to her hips and thighs, and I need to swallow before saying anything to her.

"Ms. Goodridge, good morning," I say, keeping my voice even.

A few other parents are walking with their children around us. Ms. Goodridge waves at one of them, the gold bangles on her arm jingling.

My eyes walk up her arm and settle on her chest before looking away hurriedly. I need to get a hold of myself.

"How was your weekend?" I ask, clearing my throat.

Mia lays her bright green gaze on me.

"Boring. I could definitely use something to... do." she says with a gleam in her eyes.

My heart beats a little faster as I shift from foot to foot. I'm keenly aware of the dozens of other people around us. Any one of them could be watching.

The shrill ringing of the school bell from inside the building pulls Ms. Goodridge's attention away from me for a moment, allowing me to breathe. Glancing back at me, she places her hand on my arm to say goodbye.

"And so it begins. Bye for now—don't be a stranger," she says, adding the second part in a lower tone that only I can hear.

Her fingers remain on my arm a second longer than they probably should have. Then she's moving toward the school, leaving me to *try* not to watch after her as she walks away in that skirt.

I try to shake myself out of it. We swore we'd never do anything like that again, and yet here she goes.

Turning, I begin to step into the street before the horn of an oncoming car freezes me. It continues to blare as the car moves by, and I raise a hand in apology before crossing after it passes.

Mia and I can't happen. Not again.

I don't know what would happen to me if Judith found out.

THREE
JUDITH

I pull my eyes from the skyline view as our apartment door swings open behind me.

A quick glance down at my smart watch tells me Mark's running a little late this morning. Usually I've just pulled on my pantsuit jacket when I hear him coming in after picking up Amelia.

I suppose if I wanted things to be a little more prompt, I could be the one to drive over to my sisters to pick up Amelia after the weekend... but then there's the issue of having to see my sister.

After everything she's done to me and Mark, that's about the last thing in the world I'd like to do.

In fact, the last words I spoke to her were telling her that the next time we saw each other, it'd be at her funeral.

So, Mark does pick up and drop-offs. I guess that means I need to give him a little leeway on timing.

"Cutting it close," I say, tapping my watch face as I

step away from our floor-to-ceiling windows and set down my cup of coffee on the counter.

I'm dressed and ready. My hair has already been straightened, not a strand out of place. Appearance is everything, especially for a woman. If you want people to take you seriously, you've got to dress seriously.

That's something I've been trying to instill in Amelia. It's never too early to learn these things.

Mark gives me a shrug, which irks me just a little. "Sorry. Katie was a little slow coming to the door."

I pause mid stride and look back at him, an eyebrow raised. "Did—"

"She swore up and down she hadn't been drinking," Mark says, cutting me off, "but... I don't know. She looked a little rough."

A huff of air escapes my throat.

"I knew this *changed woman* thing wouldn't stick," I say, shaking my head.

It sounds harsh, but it's simply the truth. I've been Katie's sister for thirty-three years after all.

Time and time again, she has proven to me she cannot be trusted. With anything.

That's the way it has always been, and that's the way it'll always be.

Despite knowing that, she almost had me convinced this time. Over two years without any sort of issue, but it was always just a matter of time.

Mark says nothing, moving past me to the fridge where I've got his lunch packed for him. As I said, appearance is everything, so I take great care in deciding what goes into our bodies.

As we age, our diets become even more important in maintaining a healthy, youthful figure.

With his lunchbox in hand, Mark glances up at me. "Ready to go?"

I check my watch and then nod. Almost seven minutes behind our usual schedule. If this negatively affects our commute, I won't be pleased.

After picking up my own lunchbox, I follow Mark as we walk through the apartment toward the front door again.

My eyes flick up to the second-floor balcony as I pass underneath, realizing that I've left my bedroom door open.

"One moment," I say, not waiting for Mark to respond before I stride up the glass and metal spiral staircase to the second floor.

I know I'm making us even later, but if everything isn't in its rightful place, it's going to bother me all day. Reaching the door, I close it the final couple inches, the satisfying click music to my ears.

Now we can leave.

Mark is looking up at me as I descend the spiral stairs.

"What?"

He shakes his head. "Nothing."

For a moment I consider pressing him on it but decide against it. His tardiness and mine cancel each other out in my mind, and as I see it, the field is even. No need to change that before nine in the morning. I work best with a clear head, after all.

Together we exit the apartment and head for the

elevator, our dress shoes stepping quietly over the lush hallway carpet. It takes almost thirty seconds of waiting before an elevator car becomes available.

That gets my face a little warm, and I feel Mark shift beside me. I don't acknowledge it, but I can feel his eyes on me as we step inside and start down.

We step out of the elevator and into the parking garage, which is below our building. A parking spot in here costs just over a thousand dollars a month, but it's well worth it. For me, owning a vehicle is a must. After all, what alternative is there really?

I certainly won't step foot in the subway—that filthy, faulty, disease-ridden cesspool.

Mark tosses me the keys from his pocket as we head toward our car. I chose black for the color, because it's harder to see any dirty marks. I click the door unlock button on the fob, and the car responds.

Getting behind the wheel, I run my hands over the top of the steering wheel leather and then flick my eyes up to the rearview mirror. There's no one behind us, so I back the car out of its spot, and we get moving.

It's only once we ease to a stop at the parking garage entrance and I flick on the turn signal that I realize Mark has barely spoken to me all morning.

A glance over at him doesn't reveal much. He's looking out the passenger window, hands clasped in front of him. The cuff on his left sleeve is slightly wrinkled.

"What's on your mind?" I ask.

Mark pulls himself away from the window to look back at me. "Nothing, really. Thinking about Katie, I guess."

I shake my head again. My big sister. The *fun* Rose sister, people used to say.

No one says that anymore.

"If she's drinking again, we'll know soon enough," I respond with a short nod.

She can never hide it for long.

"And if she is, we're going to do what we discussed," I finish.

Mark nods solemnly. The car falls back into silence.

I can tell Mark wants to turn on the radio, but he knows my rule about that. When I drive, there are no distractions. In this city, even the smallest thing could spell disaster, and I'm very careful about staving off disaster.

Both of us work in Midtown, though my building is closer to the parking garage. As we pull up to Mark's building, I put the car into park and turn on my hazard lights. Mark leans across the center console and we do our obligatory peck-kiss before he slides out of the car with a goodbye.

As he opens the door, I'm met with a sharp rush of cool air. It's refreshing. A sign that any semblance of summer has finally departed.

I've always been a fan of the cold more than the heat. Sticky sweat has never been something I've enjoyed. Mark shuts his door and steps up onto the sidewalk to head into his building.

As he goes, I can't help but admire his profile. Tall and muscular, with a strong head of hair for his age. I've done well picking out his clothing, too. His pants and suit jacket fit his frame perfectly.

My husband disappears into the throng of bodies on the sidewalk, and I put the car back into drive again. It's only another couple minutes' drive to the parking garage.

Now that I'm alone, I can't stop my thoughts from drifting back to my sister, as much as I wished they wouldn't. I had to put on a strong face in front of Mark, but the thought of her drinking again has my chest tightening.

Last time was bad enough. So bad in fact, that at some points, I wondered whether we were in danger. The notes she sent certainly made it appear so.

Pulling into a parking spot, I shut off the engine and allow myself one final moment before taking in a large breath and opening the door.

At least I have Mark.

Even in all the craziness, I know I can always count on him, despite his idiosyncrasies.

FOUR

KATIE

The pint glasses clink in my hand as I grab hold of all four of them, clearing the table.

Poking out of the check holder is my tip, the edges of the cash a little damp from the excess water on the table. I flip the book open with my free hand, and my heart falls.

Six dollars. A six-buck tip on a bill of over seventy dollars.

My eyes move around the dimly lit bar, but there's no sign of the two finance guys who were just seated here on their lunch break. Was it my service?

Admittedly, I was a little slow getting them that second round of beers. But I've just been so scatter-brained over the past few days.

It's got to be my sleep—or lack of it. I don't know what's going on, but it's like my body no longer wants to turn off, even when I'm utterly exhausted.

I was tossing and turning for hours last night, my brain running wild with every nightmare scenario I could possibly dream up. All the while, the quiet whispers in my mind.

A way to make it all go away, to quiet everything.

The urge to drink has been more insistent as of late. I thought it was supposed to get easier the longer you go without.

But I won't give in. I swore to Mark that I wouldn't, and I have to hold myself to that, as tough as it is. Well, discounting that little sip I had.

But that was it—just one tiny sip from the bottle before I tossed it.

So I pocket the six dollars and deposit the empty glasses in the tiny kitchen adjacent to the bar. Seeing as not many people want to slam beers at one in the afternoon, the owners figured they'd start selling food, too. Ostensibly that meant the tips were going to be larger, but clearly that isn't always the case.

Now that the stingy vest-wearing finance guys are gone, there are only a couple other patrons in the place. Stevie is in the back flipping burgers and doing the dishes whenever he gets a chance. I position myself behind the bar again, head still feeling sluggish as I put the check holder back with the others.

There's a nagging feeling I can't quite seem to place. Did I forget to bring the guys something? Maybe that's why they stiffed me on the tip.

The door swings inward, admitting a golden ray of fall sun into the dark bar. It's Lucy, a fellow bartender who's practically half my age.

She's super early, though. I'm on until six, and it's

just after three PM right now. Guess she needs the money just as badly as I do.

I reorganize the menus as Lucy comes up to the bar. As she does, I notice she's looking at me funny.

"Sorry I'm late," she says. "The subway just like... didn't move once we hit West 4th."

I stare blankly at her for a moment. Late? But she's...

My heart thuds hard, hard enough that it's actually painful. *Oh no.*

It's Friday. I'm supposed to be picking Amelia up from school today, which lets out at...

2:45.

My throat tightens. I'm so late. So, so late.

How could I have forgotten about that? I shoot out from behind the bar in a flurry of movement, my limbs feeling jittery as I yank off my apron and stumble for the door.

My thoughts race as I go, creating nightmare visuals to match. Amelia standing there outside the school, waiting and waiting and waiting.

Waiting for Mommy, who has somehow forgotten about her. I feel sick to my stomach, the knot so tight I can hardly breathe.

How could I do this? The tiredness, the sluggishness... but it's no excuse.

Bursting out into the sunshine, I whip my head around, searching my panic-addled brain for the direction I need to turn for the subway. All I can picture is Amelia standing out there in front of the empty school, her little face crumpled in despair. I can't believe this.

My legs are wobbly as I practically sprint down the

sidewalk, shooting past people in a flurry of commotion. The train seems to take forever to come, my foot jack-hammering against the station's tile floor.

Every second that passes is another second I'm not there.

When the Bordley School finally comes into view, I'm a sweaty, jittery mess. I've been running flat out for almost a quarter of a mile, my lungs burning and shoulders heaving.

There are the red school doors up ahead... but no Amelia.

Blinking hard, I scramble up the stone steps and slip inside the building. The cool air-conditioning does little to relieve the heat that seems to be seeping out of every pour of my being from the sprint.

I'm nearly doubled over in the lobby, gasping for oxygen as I try to recover when I hear my name.

"Katie?"

I shoot upright. *Mark.*

He's standing beside one of the schoolteachers, his hands on Amelia's shoulders. As I look down at my daughter's face, I see her eyes are bleary, streaked red. That splits my heart in two.

"Baby, I'm so sorry," I say, still a bit breathless, "Mommy completely lost track of time."

The teacher, a pretty blonde woman, moves away from Mark to give the three of us some privacy.

Amelia sniffs as Mark looks me up and down. I've recovered enough now that I can stand up straight and squeeze my core so my chest stops heaving so much.

Mark chews the inside of his lip for a second before looking down at Amelia.

"Why don't you show Mrs. MacIntosh in the office your beautiful drawing. I'm sure she wants to see it," he says. "Mommy and Daddy need to have a quick talk."

Amelia glances up at me for a moment before nodding and stepping around Mark to head through the office doorway behind him.

"What happened?" he asks, taking a step forward.

I shake my head, rubbing my face. "I just... I got caught up at work. But I came as soon as I could."

"You left her here alone for almost an hour, Katie. I had to leave work to come get her," Mark says.

His voice is a low hiss. I look through the sliding glass panels of the office at our daughter. She's showing the receptionist her drawing. The woman smiles widely and says what a good job she did. My heart pangs.

I should be the one doing that. I should've been here.

"I'm sorry," I say, my eyes brimming with tears, "I... I... there's no excuse."

I can't take it back, and that's the worst part. I can't take any of it back.

"There really isn't. Forgetting your own daughter," Mark says with a shake of his head, his arms crossed.

Then he leans in toward me and sniffs the air. I blink hard, the tears giving way to anger.

"I'm not drinking again," I say loudly.

Too loudly. Defensively loud, but there's just so much emotion flowing through me right now, and I can't...

I blink again. The receptionist's eyes are on me.

Amelia's too. It's her expression that hurts the most as our eyes meet through the glass.

Mark breathes out heavily as he rubs his forehead. "I'm taking Amelia home today. I think the reason should be obvious. I'll bring her to your place tomorrow. You should start figuring out how you're going to apologize to her."

I nod numbly.

His gaze washes over me. "You need to figure yourself out, Katie. I mean it. You're out of chances."

"Chances to–" I start, but Mark has already turned away and stepped into the office to retrieve Amelia. He hoists her up onto his shoulders, making her giggle.

"Here we go, setting sail. Ready, Captain?" he asks our little girl, who giggles again.

They come out of the office and back into the school entryway.

"Mommy and I had a little mix-up today, that's all," Mark says to Amelia as he comes to a stop in front of me.

"A little confusion, but it won't happen again. Right Mommy?" he asks, looking at me.

I nod quickly, stepping forward to grab hold of Amelia's hands. From her position on Mark's shoulders, I have to look up at her to meet her gaze. It takes me a second to connect with her eyes, but finally I do.

"I'm so, so sorry baby. It won't ever happen again, okay?" I say, to which Amelia nods, but she isn't fully looking at me anymore.

"How about I take all day tomorrow to make it up to you? We could go to the Natural History Museum, maybe the park. How about that?"

This time, Amelia looks directly at me. She smiles and nods, and I give her small hands a squeeze.

"Okay. I'll see you tomorrow then. I love you sweetheart," I say, still holding her hand until I'm forced to drop it as Mark begins to head toward the street.

He gives me one final look before stepping out, letting out a pirate *ARGH* that has Amelia in a fit of giggles.

I remain rooted to the tile as I watch them go. I can't afford to take tomorrow off, but it doesn't matter. My daughter means more to me than anything, so I'll just have to find a way.

There's nothing I wouldn't do not to lose her.

FIVE
MARK

I shouldn't be doing this.

I know that. I really do. But between Katie and Judith, I just need a break. Some semblance of normalcy, even if just for the night.

Amelia is with Katie right now, and Judith's at work. She's always in-office on Saturdays, which has been the case for years.

I know it's not, but it almost feels like a green light from the Universe for doing what I'm about to do.

Mia gives me her trademark smirk as she appears in the doorway of her apartment building.

I took the subway up, as Judith keeps track of the car miles. There's no way Mia and I could go back to my place, because knowing my wife, I wouldn't be surprised if there were hidden sensors or something to detect heat signatures a degree out of the usual.

Mia pushes open the door and greets me with a wink.

"Been far too long since our last parent-teacher conference."

She's wearing that pair of thin wire-framed glasses she knows I love. And even though it's a Saturday, she's got on a gorgeous dress, too. It moves in sync with her as she shifts to invite me inside the building.

I let out a cough and rub my hands together. Now that the sun sets so early, the temperature has really started to drop.

My eyes scan the familiar interior of her slightly dingy apartment building. There was a time I swore I'd never see those pinkish-red tiles again.

Swallowing the uncomfortable feeling that begins to bubble up in my stomach, I reach into my vest and pull out a bottle of red wine like a magician pulling a rabbit from a hat.

"For you," I say with a smile that smothers that nagging feeling in my chest.

Between Katie's apparent relapse and Judith's ever-increasing demands, I feel almost ready to snap. Pretty much the only person in my life who doesn't want something from me is Mia.

With her, it's all about giving. She gives freely, and even though I know it's wrong, I just can't get enough.

We giggle and kiss as we move down the hallway to the staircase along the back wall. She lives on the sixth floor—no elevator—which means my legs are absolutely burning by the time we finally make it up there.

Various noises reach my ears as we ascend the floors. Shouts, laughter, sounds of a party. An early Saturday evening getting underway in New York City.

And here I am, cheating on my wife. Again.

The door to Mia's apartment clicks shut behind me.

She turns around to face me, half-illuminated by the living room lamp that glows behind her.

"Are you coming?" she asks jokingly, wiggling the bottle of wine in her hand like a lure on a hook.

Swallowing, I nod and slip off my shoes to put them on the rack with the rest. Her roommates are out of town for the weekend, a fact she shared with me yesterday when I arrived to pick up Amelia.

I should've just nodded and moved on with the conversation, but I didn't. The way she was looking at me, touching my arm... it was a promise of much more than flirtation.

Something I haven't had in nearly six months now.

"You know, as much as I wanted this to happen, I was actually a little surprised to get your text," Mia says, looking over her shoulder at me as she reaches up to the cabinet for a couple wine glasses.

I plop down on her L-shaped couch with a huff.

"I feel like I remember you saying something along the lines of, 'we can't do this anymore,'" she says playfully.

After opening the bottle and pouring, Mia steps over to me with two wine glasses in hand, one of which she extends out to me. I take it and gulp down a good mouthful of alcohol before responding.

"Well, that was then. This is now," I say, running a hand through my hair as I relax back into the couch cushions.

Mia reaches out a hand and runs it up the length of my forearm. "She's really getting to you, huh?"

I scoff. "Which one?"

Then I shake my head. "I don't really want to talk about all that nonsense. It'd probably bore you anyway."

Now it's Mia's turn to shake her head. "Of course I want to hear about what's bothering you. I care about you, and that means I care about what you care about," she says.

She takes a seat on the couch next to me and slides up close. Our outer thighs touch, and it makes my heart beat faster. I don't think she's taken her gaze off me for a second since I walked in here.

The undivided attention is flattering. It feels good.

"I'm just... I can't be everything for everyone all the time, you know?" I say finally, letting it out in a rush.

"I just... I just need a break."

Mia smirks. "And you do deserve one. No one works harder than you or does more for others than you do."

I sit up a little higher on the couch, nodding. "Exactly. Feels like I can't ever think about me, you know, and what *I* want to do, how *I* want to live."

Mia puts her hand on my leg as she takes a long sip of her wine. "Maybe you need to be with someone who cares about things like that."

I pause with my wine glass mid-drink.

What exactly is she insinuating?

She laughs. "Wow, this wine is really running through me. I haven't eaten anything all day."

"Judith has just been driving me nuts lately," I say. "We're going to this pumpkin patch with Amelia next week, but you'd think we're going to the moon, the way she's preparing."

Mia polishes off her glass of wine. "Tell Judy—"

"Judith," I say, interrupting her, "Judy is too childish, she says."

"Tell *Judy* to chill out. Fall should be about fun."

Shaking my head, I gulp down another mouthful of wine before speaking.

"You'd think so, wouldn't you? I used to think like that, too. Then I came to understand just how much effort goes into making everything look effortless."

By the time I finish speaking, Mia has climbed into my lap and is now sitting astride me, her face just a few inches from mine. Her bright eyes remain locked on mine as she bites her lower lip.

"Then let me help make it easier," she says, her voice barely above a whisper.

Our lips press together in a kiss that gets me more than riled up. Any inner reluctance I had before seems to dissipate like smoke as we connect.

Afterward, I'm left staring up at Mia's bedroom ceiling.

Satisfied. And terrified.

Ashamed.

My hand runs over Mia's bare shoulder as she snuggles up against me. I swallow, feeling my Adam's apple travel up and down. I can hear the noise of my swallow in the silence of her room.

Judith gets off work soon, which means I can't be here much longer.

"I'm so glad you reached out," Mia murmurs from somewhere down my chest.

I remain staring at the ceiling, unblinking. "Me too."

Mia giggles again. "You said Judith is a real stickler—what would she do if she saw us here, like this?"

I scoff, but my stomach tightens.

"What, shattering the illusion of our perfect life together? I honestly think she might kill me," I say.

Mia chuckles and rolls over, taking it as a joke.

Really, I'm only partly joking.

SIX

JUDITH

I've already changed out of my work clothes and into my downtime outfit when I hear the front door click open and then shut quietly.

Striding out of the bedroom, I nearly run into Mark as he rounds the corner. He practically jumps out of his skin, eyes going wide before he untenses himself.

"Scared me. Didn't think you were home yet," he says with a chuckle.

"They let us off a couple minutes early," I say. "What have you been up to?"

Mark nudges his chin back toward the door. "Went for a walk. No good games on tonight, and I didn't feel like sitting alone in an empty house."

I tap my foot. "Did you bring your pepper spray?"

Mark's breath catches in his throat for a moment before he shakes his head no. "Forgot it. Sorry."

I chew my lip. "I'd really like for you to try and remember it, okay? In this city, anything can happen, so it's better to be prepared."

It's the truth. I've made sure to put prep-packs in our car, as well as Mark's mother's car since she sometimes babysits Amelia for us. She might think it's dumb to keep pepper spray in the car, but I know better.

Anything can happen, and I'd rather be prepared than not.

Mark is nodding as he starts to move past me into the bedroom.

"Right. I'll try and remember next time," he says.

He strips off his shirt and pants to take a shower and wash off any residual sweat from the walk. That much I appreciate, because he knows how I feel about sweat and body odor.

I leave him to it, heading into the living room to turn on the television. The city outside our apartment is dark and looming, save for the yellow glow spilling out from lit windows. I've always preferred New York at night.

Probably because in the dark, it's harder to see the grime.

The master bath shower hisses to life from the other room as I settle onto the couch. There's a faint but noticeable dark spot on the fabric of the cushion beside me. Amelia must've spilled something on it again, even though she knows better.

I let out a small breath. I've got to cut her some slack. She's only five, after all, and it isn't like she's doing it on purpose.

When I bring it to her attention, I'll be as kind as I can.

Even still, I can't fully relax knowing the stain is just

sitting right there beside me. Practically glowing like someone is shining a spotlight on it.

Eventually, I can't stand it anymore and get up from the couch to head into the kitchen for cleaning supplies. The stain is gone by the time Mark comes out of the bedroom all freshly cleaned and slightly pink.

"What're you doing?" he asks.

"Stain," I say, grunting as I give it a final rub.

Mark nods silently and pads into the kitchen.

"Tomorrow would be a good day to see about getting your shirt ironed," I say, the thought popping into my head.

We aren't going to the pumpkin patch until next week, but it never hurts to be prepared. Giving ourselves plenty of days to do so is also always a good idea.

"Right," Mark says from the kitchen.

"And what did you think of the outfit I picked out? I think I want red to be our color this year," I say.

"Yeah. Good," he replies after a second.

I hear the fridge door open, and then a crack as he breaks the seal on a new bottle of wine.

I sit back, satisfied. I've been looking forward to this fall trip since the start of the year. It's taken me just about that long to iron out what I want the pictures to look like, though I've finally decided.

A warm feeling washes through my chest as I think of the upcoming trip. Our little family, swapping the hustle and bustle of the city for the crisp clean upstate air.

In the cutest coordinated outfits you've ever seen. Not matchy-matchy—certainly not—but just similar enough to satisfy the eye.

Try as Katie might, she won't get to ruin it, either. Whatever is going on with her is just going to have to go on without us, and I'm completely okay with that at this point.

I've worked extremely hard to get where I am. Granted, I started with the sizeable inheritance from Mom and Dad when they passed, but I could've burned through it like my sister. Now, she's worth more dead than alive.

Unlike her, I invested well, and that nest egg is now a much larger one.

I earned this. Seated here on this designer couch in an apartment that costs more than most monthly salaries. A handsome husband in the other room.

A beautiful little girl.

Some of those things were Katie's, once. If she wanted to keep them, she should've worked harder. Like me.

There's no doubt we'll get plenty of likes on social media with our fall posts. A smile touches my face as Mark comes back in with a glass of wine.

It's been a long road, and more work than I originally envisioned, but finally, *finally*, I have the perfect life.

SEVEN

KATIE

I'm a mess.

I have been all week, after what happened last Friday. Even though I'm pretty sure Amelia's forgiven me, I haven't been able to forgive myself. Just inexcusable.

My sleep schedule somehow seems to be even more off-kilter. I'm not sure why.

Maybe it's because I'm so terrified I'm going to forget something else. My brain simply doesn't want to shut off at night. Then I'm so exhausted, I sleep late into the day.

Yesterday I woke up, and it was actually dark out already. I slept through the entirety of the daylight and spent every waking hour in darkness.

I doesn't help that I can't seem to get Mark's words out of my mind.

You're out of chances.

That phrase has been stuck in my brain all week, my thoughts churning and boiling over each other.

Chances to what?

That's what I want to know. It wasn't just the words themselves—it was the way he said them. There was a terrifying finality to them that still makes my chest tighten up when I think back to it.

I let out a shaking breath and run a hand through my hair. My fingertips come back shiny. I can't remember the last time I washed my hair properly. It's just been pass out, work, stew in my thoughts. Hours pass as I lie there in the dark.

Today is Thursday. I think. The grainy window over my sink reveals darkness outside the windows, though a look at the clock tells me it's just after six.

I don't work today, which means there is absolutely nothing for me to do.

The idea of sitting here marinating in my own thoughts again for the umpteenth day in a row is nauseating. What I need is some fresh air. A walk to clear my head.

Grabbing my coat off its hook, I slip my arms into the sleeves and pull up the zipper. A siren wails from somewhere outside, though it's distant enough to be little more than a faint cry.

My shoes squeak on the tile hallway floor as I head toward the building's front door. Stepping out, I understand why. A light spatter of rain flitters down, the drops little more than mist in the night air.

I don't feel like going all the way back up to my apartment, so I just head out. Pretty sure this jacket is waterproof, anyhow. Or at least it was when I bought it a few years ago.

The streets around me are dead. Everything shines

from the misting precipitation. Cars lie dormant on both sides of the street. The door closes behind me, and then I'm headed down the sidewalk, pushing out little puffs of air.

Some exercise will do me good. Maybe if I can really tire myself out, I'll actually be able to go to sleep at a decent hour tonight. With my hands stuffed into my jacket pockets, I start off in a random direction.

Soon enough I end up at the subway station and decide on a whim to get on a train. Not even sure where this one is going. I just want to see life right now, distraction, and where I live in Brooklyn is not the place.

Here, it's just me and my thoughts.

Maybe if I'm surrounded by thousands of other people I'll finally be able to give my brain a rest. Just blend in with the rest of humanity, pretend for a few minutes I'm just like the rest of them.

Normal, with somewhere to go. People to see.

Everyone on the train is bundled up like me. All of us sitting silently surrounded by layers of fabric. Deep in my jacket, I can be anyone. No one knows it's really me, not with the hood up.

I get off at some stop and make my way above ground again, this time in the company of several others.

They shoot off in all directions, moving with purpose. I amble forward without one, having to forcefully look away from a large liquor store sign that looms overhead.

My mouth dries slightly, and I pick up my pace.

Not tonight. As tough as dealing with my thoughts is, the last thing I need right now is to silence them with a bottle.

No, I'm clearing my head. Not clouding it.

I'm not sure how much time has passed, but the next time I look up, I realize I'm actually in Mark's neighborhood. His apartment is just a couple streets over.

How did I get here?

It's not like I picked out this destination on purpose. I didn't even know where I was going.

Now that I'm here though, the urge to just... walk by his apartment is strong. Just to see if anything is going on, that's all.

I'm not stalking them or anything. My daughter is there right now, and I guess I just want to be closer to her.

My feet carry me in the direction of the apartment as a cold breeze blows down the street. Even with my jacket on, it seems to cut through me in a way that makes me shiver.

At least the rain has pretty much stopped, now little more than a shine on the street that reflects the glow of the lights around me. As the stoplight changes from red to green, I see the colors reflected in the sheen.

Mark lives in a very nice building. I guess that makes sense, since he and Judith both have very good jobs. It's the kind of place with a front desk and a doorman who keeps track of everyone coming and going.

Part of me wonders if they moved here because of me.

My stomach twists at that as I think about what they told me I did last time.

I don't remember any of it, but even hearing it secondhand left me wracked with guilt.

But I'm different now. For real this time.

I'm not sure what exactly my plan is here, seeing as they live on one of the upper floors not remotely visible from the street. I come to a stop across the street from the building, sitting down on the edge of a large cement planter.

Whatever it held has shriveled up from the change in temperature. The edge is damp, wetting the seat of my pants instantly as I come up against it.

My eyes move back to the building across the street. My daughter and husband are in there right now, and I am not.

As the thought rolls over me, I feel that nagging voice in the back of my head again. Whispering in my ear as the thought seeps in.

I know how to make these worries go away.

I chew my lip. Amelia won't be coming by until Saturday. No one would know if I drank just a little. Just enough to make all these regrets quiet down.

After all, it's been years. I can stop, I've showed that, haven't I?

And yet here I am, sitting out here in the damp night alone while my husband and child are cozy and snug up in their lovely tower.

I should be up there with them, and I'm not sure if I'm more sad or angry that I'm not.

EIGHT

MARK

I tap my hand on the wall.

"Let's go, Captain. Ship's ready to sail," I call toward Amelia's room.

"Coming," Amelia answers from somewhere within her room.

My fingers run along the inside of the flannel collar of my shirt. It's stiff and starchy, and almost feels like it's scratching me, though I can't feel anything sticking out. I drop my hand as Judith rounds the staircase.

"What's the hold up?" she asks.

Her voice is tense, which automatically makes me tense.

Amelia appears on que, taking a step down the hallway before quickly turning and shutting her bedroom door. Judith smiles in approval, and then we're all headed down the stairs.

Today is the big day, and Amelia's very excited. That should be enough to get me into the fall spirit, but after Mia's texts last night, I'm having trouble relaxing.

We've always been very careful to keep our texts very emotionless, just in case Judith were to see them.

Only last night, as I was tucking Amelia into bed, Mia sent me a message that set my pulse skyrocketing.

I want you and I don't care who knows it.

Well, I certainly care.

She's always seemed into me, but there's something different this time around. I'm not really sure how to put it into words... maybe bolder.

She's bolder now than before, which I'm not crazy about at all.

Like this text. I deleted it immediately, my heart in my throat. If Judith were to see that text from JOE WORK PHONE, she'd obviously have questions.

All I wanted was a break from stress. Instead, it seems I just went ahead and ordered an extra helping.

Then again, I did make this bed, so I suppose it's only fair I have to lie in it. No one forced me to sleep with Mia. I came up with that brilliant idea myself, and now I'm paying for it.

It's been almost twelve hours, and Mia hasn't texted again, or asked why I didn't respond. I'm hoping it stays that way, because I've got to be present with Judith and Amelia today.

At least things seem to be settling down with Katie. After last weekend's debacle, I was preparing for the worst. Angry texts, notes, you name it.

It's been quiet, though. Amelia said Katie was wonderful on Saturday and Sunday, which is good.

I'll guess I'll know more when I drop her off tomorrow. Pushing all of that out of mind, I prop a smile on my face as we head for the elevator. Judith is halfway through laying out the order of the photographs she wants to take, so I nod.

The elevator lets us out in the parking garage, and together we head in the direction of the car. Amelia is practically bubbling over with excitement—probably because I promised her as much candy corn as she could eat.

"...and then we'll probably have to pay the farm extra to position the hay to our liking, but I think it's worth it," Judith says.

"Absolutely," I say with another nod.

There's the car up ahead. I'm driving today, and I pull the keys from my pocket to unlock the doors.

As we come up on the car however, I spot something sitting on the hood. Judith sees it at the same time as me, and both of us stop in place.

There's a can of beer sitting there. I take another step, glancing back and forth as I approach the can. Picking it up, I find it's nearly empty.

"I don't believe it," Judith says sharply.

I don't need to be a mind reader to know what she's thinking. *Katie.*

"I've been saying for months they need to fix security in this garage. Literally all you have to do is duck under the arm, and you're in. I just don't believe it," Judith adds.

I lift the can from the hood and look around for a trash can.

"We don't know it was her," I say.

Judith scoffs. "Right. It was probably my *other* alcoholic stalker sister who wants my life."

My eyes shoot down to Amelia, who's looking between the two of us. I catch Judith's eye and signal with a raised brow and a slight head tilt toward my daughter that she should cool it on the blame game in front of the child.

Judith lets out an irritated sigh.

"I'm gonna have them review the security tape. If it's her, I'm pressing charges," she says with finality.

With that, she yanks open her car door and slips inside.

I open Amelia's door and scoop her up to get her into her booster seat.

"Was Mommy here?" she asks in her sweet little voice.

"We're not sure," I say, my gaze meeting Judith's.

My wife turns around in her seat, but doesn't say anything.

"But who is ready for some apple cider?" I ask, my voice picking up.

Amelia cheers, and I give her a big smile, though it drops as soon as I move away from her and close her door.

If Katie *was* here, and was drinking that beer, that is not good at all. So much for things looking up. I rub my face with a hand before pulling open my door and piling into the car.

I get it started, the sound of the engine revving to life joining the happy sound of Amelia chattering away excitedly in the backseat.

As I pull out of the parking spot however, I'm not thinking about candied apples and corn mazes.

I'm thinking about my ex-wife, and wondering what's going to happen next.

NINE
JUDITH

I'm extremely pleased with the weather today.

We couldn't have asked for a better day. A crisp fifty-five degrees, with no wind and low humidity. Absolutely ideal for a fall photoshoot—and for my hair, which I spent considerable time on this morning.

If only I could focus entirely on the photo itinerary. Instead, I've got to worry now about my sister.

Mark didn't seem convinced it was actually her that left that can on the car, but I know better.

The moment I saw it, I knew. It wasn't a brand I remember her drinking, but that doesn't matter. Water from any well is still water to a person dying of thirst.

I knew it was too good to last. All that talk about changing, and here we are again. Almost feels like deja-vu in a way, only significantly worse, because now it means I've got to start thinking about what might come next.

This day was supposed to be about us, our wonderful family, and instead I've got to spend brain power worrying about my degenerate older sister. Mark appears similarly pre-occupied, though he's doing his best to hide it.

We've just finished up our first couple of photos, with the corn in the background as we sit on hay bales with pumpkins around us. It turned out well, but I don't get the burst of satisfaction I was hoping for. I've got too much else on the brain.

As I direct us toward the barn for our next one, I notice Mark give a look at his phone and type out a quick message before pocketing it. That's the third time he's done that today.

He looks up to find me already looking at him.

"Work thing. Apparently not everyone got the message I took today off," he says with a little smile.

"Well, this is family time, so try to keep it to a minimum, okay?" I say with a tight-lipped smile.

Mark nods. "Of course. Should be all set now."

Good. Now we can get back to doing what we all came here to do. I get everything ready for the next shot, having to call over one of the farm hands so he can close the barn doors to cover up the farm equipment inside.

Amelia does well, sitting nicely in her dress as I take the photos. Once I'm satisfied, it's time to do the corn maze. I'm not looking forward to it, having to walk through such a mess, but Mark promised Amelia we'd all do it together, so I change my shoes back at the car and then we head off into the stalks of corn.

There are a few other people starting the maze with us, though they divert away at the first turn, leaving the three of us standing at a crossroads. Two paths forward.

"Which do you think we should take, Cap'n?" Mark asks Amelia.

She points to the left and starts walking toward it.

"This one," she squeaks.

Mark follows after her. After another moment, I follow too.

I'm not sure who came to the conclusion that getting lost on purpose was fun, but I strongly disagree.

It feels like we've been walking for hours, though in reality it's probably been about ten minutes. It smells like manure, too. Remind me to toss these shoes when we get back home.

I breathe through my mouth as much as I am able as we venture further into the tall walls of corn. The sky overhead is a brilliant blue, with bulbous clouds drifting by that obscure the sun for seconds at a time.

"What about this way? I feel like we've already been down there," Mark says, directing Amelia to our right.

"No, we haven't. That's a new path," I say irritably.

The stench of cow poop is starting to get to me. Mark gives me a look.

"Are you okay?" he asks in a low voice.

"How much longer do you think this'll be?" I ask.

Mark's jaw tightens.

"I don't know, Judith. About as long as my daughter wants it to be, I guess," he says before walking away from me to catch up to Amelia.

I want to retort, but a rustling from within the corn stalks stops me. My gaze darts in the direction of the noise—somewhere behind me. Mark and Amelia are already steps ahead, laughing with each other.

My eyes remain on the corn. That wasn't just the wind, was it?

I'm getting myself worked up for nothing. Shaking my head, I take another step forward—only to hear another rustle.

This time, I'm sure it wasn't the breeze. My heartbeat picks up as I try and peer through the thick stalks.

"Hello? Is someone there?" I ask, my mouth suddenly a little dry.

There's no response.

Even still, I can't shake the feeling like I'm being watched or something. It makes the hairs on my arms raise slightly, and I take a few quick steps to catch up to Mark and Amelia, my hands a little shaky.

I'm getting myself all bent out of shape over nothing, I know it. I also know why.

That beer can on the car. Try as I might, I just can't seem to get Katie's stalkerish behavior out of my mind. But no, she wouldn't follow us all the way out here.

She doesn't even have a car. Can't afford it, and that's probably for the best. Mark's back comes into view in front of me. He's got Amelia hoisted up on his shoulders so she can try and see above the corn.

I let out a short breath, forcefully releasing any pent-up, nagging feelings with it.

As I do, I realize I've been a little too militant with everyone today, an unconscious overcorrection after this morning's find.

Some part of me almost seems to want to prove how unlike my sister I am, even at the cost of my relationships.

I'm here with my family, which means I should be here mentally, too.

"That might be considered cheating," I say, a wry smile crossing my face as I come up to them.

Mark spins, grinning. I can tell I said the right thing, because any traces of the irritation on his face from my earlier comments have disappeared. So, with another deep breath, I allow Amelia to lead us in circles through the corn for another hour or so.

It actually ends up being more entertaining than I expected, and by the end of it, I'm a little shocked to find I'm actually enjoying the experience. When we finally do manage to find the exit, I've got a genuine smile on my face.

We accomplished something, and we did it together.

Upon seeing the exit back out into the farm, Amelia lets out a cheer and sprints forward. Mark and I follow her. He buys plenty of candy corn and other sugary garbage at the farmhouse stalls, but I don't make a comment. Most of it is for Amelia, anyway.

Once the sugar has been consumed, we take a ride around the farm grounds on a trailer pulled by an old tractor and even older farmer. I point out the various animals to Amelia, who delights in listing off their names and a few fun facts for each one.

She's definitely intelligent, there's no doubt about that.

It makes me even more certain we made the right decision with her schooling. Really, our parenting of her in general. I look back at Mark, hoping to catch his gaze, when I see he's got his phone pulled out again by his side.

He's typing out a text with one hand, chin tucked into his chest.

I glance away before he looks up, trying to focus on what Amelia's saying, though my mind has seemingly jumped elsewhere.

The trailer bounces underneath us as we hit a bump in the uneven dirt path, eliciting a chorus of exclamations from the other riders around me.

I hardly notice, my mind instead occupied with the image of Mark on his phone. He's already told me it's work, and I'm certain that's the case.

And yet... I can't seem to let the curiosity go. Why can't I?

For whatever reason, my brain seems determined to keep thinking about that phone, even as we dismount the trailer and start making our way back to the car.

Mark is all smiles now, laughing and joking with Amelia and me. The more I think on it, the more I can't help but wonder.

I know I can be a little demanding at times, and Mark is right to call me out on that. But when he hissed at me in the corn, that was different.

What if Mark's comment wasn't so much about me and my behavior, but something else?

My throat tightens. *Someone* else.

TEN

KATIE

I shouldn't be here.

I know that. Believe me, I do. And yet here I am, huddled in my jacket and beanie resting up against the planter across the street from Mark's apartment.

I'm not sure why I'm torturing myself like this. No matter what I see, it's not going to make me feel any better.

If anything, I'll only feel a whole lot worse, having been allowed a peek into a life that should've been mine.

While not explicitly cold out, the sun setting behind the buildings has left me in a sunless patch that is considerably cooler. I experience a full-body shiver and dab at my nose with a crumpled tissue. My nose always seems to run in the cold, even when I'm not sick.

Besides a few cars entering and exiting the parking garage beneath the building, there really hasn't been much activity at their building. I don't think I've missed Mark and Amelia, though.

Today they went to the pumpkin patch upstate,

which is a bit of a drive from the city. Seeing as I know Judith hates being outside in the dark, they should be getting back any minute now.

The sky is lit up with streaks of pink that gradually shift into a purple gradient between the buildings in front of me. It's beautiful, and I wish I could focus on that and enjoy it.

But I'm unable to, my thoughts consumed instead with what could've been.

After another three minutes or so, I see a car turn onto the street at the other end. Instantly I straighten up and then shift position to retreat further into the darker recesses created by the setting sun.

That's their car. Swallowing, I latch my eyes onto it as it rolls down the road in my direction. Mark's face comes into view above the steering wheel.

He's wearing a thick flannel shirt I'm almost certain my sister picked out for him. He hates patterns like that.

Or at least, he used to. I have to remind myself I don't really know him anymore. Or myself, for that matter.

I blink hard, head on a swivel as the car rolls to a stop in front of their building.

I'm able to get a clear view of my daughter in the backseat, gesturing with excitement. Judith turns around in the passenger seat, and Mark smiles. All of it makes my chest ache.

I don't know why I came here. Did I really want to see this? To make myself feel even worse?

A happy little family—all they needed to do was sub out the old Mom for a new one.

My vision locks onto my sister. My beautiful, intelligent, perfect sister.

Everything I am not and never could be.

Her hair is absolutely perfect, as usual. Even after a day spent running around some dirty farm, she's still pristine. I feel my fingernails digging into the palm of my hand as I watch.

Maybe it's the fatigue making me think a little strangely, but I suddenly come to understand that I hate her.

Hate her for taking my husband from me. Hate her for being better than me in every conceivable way.

There's no contest between us, and that's why Mark is with her now. With my daughter in the backseat completing the happy-family-trifecta.

I focus again on Mark in the front seat.

My faithful husband. He probably had eyes for Judith the moment he first saw her, like every boyfriend I've ever had.

Everyone sees her and wants her, even if they say they don't.

Mark insisted he didn't. Every time I questioned him, which admittedly was too many times, he denied it. And yet here I am, watching him with my sister.

Another realization strikes me. I hate him even more than Judith.

I run the tissue across my nostrils again as the garage door arm comes up, and the car slips inside out of sight. It does little to quell the rising feelings in my stomach.

Anger, resentment, guilt. The guilt makes me feel

worst of all, so I stuff that down and let the anger take center stage.

They took everything from me, everything I care about.

He did that. He betrayed me. I'm out here on the straight and narrow, trying my hardest, and all I seem to get for the effort is a stern talking to and weekly humiliation.

What's the point? I'll never be my sister.

I lick my dry lips and begin to wonder if that liquor store I passed on the way here is still open.

ELEVEN

MARK

I'm first through the front door and reach to my left to flick on the lights.

The apartment is flooded with warm light as Amelia shoots past me to head into the bathroom. She still seems to be riding the sugar high from all the candy corn. I would've expected a monstrous crash by now, but somehow she's managed to escape it.

I, on the other hand, feel more than a little exhausted. My sleep last night definitely wasn't fantastic, thanks to everything going on.

Tough to count sheep when there's a million other things demanding your thoughts and attention.

Judith steps inside and instantly kicks off her shoes, which have a thin layer of mud caked onto the bottom of them. She moves for the staircase without word, but she doesn't need to say anything. I know she's headed upstairs to take a shower, wash off any semblance of dirt or sweat from the excursion.

That leaves me alone for a few seconds, and I allow

my shoulders to lower as I lean against the inside wall in the entryway, my head tipping back until I feel the wall against the crown of my head.

Mia wouldn't stop texting me the whole time I was at the farm with my family. Knowing that I was with Judith, she still didn't let up.

So much for everything blowing over. The only way I got her to stop was telling her I was going to mute her if she texted again.

I don't know what's gotten into her. It's like all of a sudden, all she can think about is me and our "relationship."

Over the past couple days, she's gone from casual fling to some clingy nightmare that has me needing to take TUMS for some relief.

It's a miracle Judith doesn't seem to suspect anything. I was pretty careful about pulling out my phone today, only doing it when I was sure she wasn't looking.

Even then, it was dangerous. I can't keep going like this. Something is going to give, and I don't know if I'll be able to handle that.

This has to stop before Judith finds out.

She can be irritating, but she's still my wife. And it's not all bad. She's got a pretty good sense of dry humor that never fails to amuse me.

I blink. What am I doing? Standing here propped up against the wall, debating the pros and cons of cheating on my wife.

What an absolute dirtbag I am.

I can only imagine what Mom would have to say to me. Pushing off the wall, I head into the kitchen for the bottle of wine I know is still in the fridge from last time. A couple of glasses should help me relax about all of this.

Just as my hand wraps around the fridge handle, the wall phone rings. It's there for the front desk to call up to the apartment and let us know when someone is here to see us.

Judith must've ordered food, and they're calling to send up the delivery guy. I don't think I saw her eat anything the whole time we were at the farm.

As I stride across the room, Judith appears at the balcony overhead, coming to a stop beside the glass panels as she looks down.

"Who is it?" she asks.

So she didn't order food. Hmm. I shrug and pick up the plastic receiver, holding it against my ear.

"Yeah," I say.

"Mr. Wharton? I've got a Mia here to see you," the voice on the other end warbles.

My stomach nearly drops out of my body, my entire frame stiffening. I blink, mouth opening but nothing coming out.

"Who is it?" Judith calls down from above.

"Mr. Wharton?" the front desk guy asks again.

"I'll be right down," I finally manage, my fingers buzzing as I stuff the phone back into its cradle on the wall.

"Mark," Judith presses.

"Package delivery," I call up to her, my mind racing, "but I didn't order anything. I'm gonna go down there and sort it out."

"Do you need–"

"Just take your shower, I'll handle it," I say, cutting her off.

My hand wraps around the door handle, and then I'm out in the hallway. The walls seem to press in from the sides as I head for the elevator.

What in the world is she doing here?

I hope my voice sounded even enough talking to Judith. Inside, every thought felt like it was screaming. Mia showed up *here*. The elevator doors ding open.

Of course, there's someone else riding in here with me. I nod to the guy, pretending everything is normal as we descend. I'm watching the floors ding by on the wall panel, but inside I'm racking my brain, trying to figure out what is going on here.

Clearly, Mia wants to talk to me. Well, this certainly isn't the way to go about it.

We hit the lobby, and I gesture for the other guy to walk out first.

It gives me another second to gather myself, and then my shoes are squeaking across the lobby floor. I reach the end of the elevator bank and turn left, which reveals the lobby in front of me.

Sure enough, Mia's blonde head of hair allows me to spot her instantly. She flashes me a big smile as she sees me, as if this is all completely normal.

"There he is," she says, nodding back to me.

The man at the front desk meets my eyes as I walk past, and I do my absolute best not to turn red. I don't know if he knows what's going on, but he looks back down at the desk regardless.

"Come here," I say, putting my hand on Mia's arm and steering us both outside.

It's definitely colder out here now that the sun is completely set. A gust of wind blows down the street, ruffling my hair as I park Mia just outside the sliding doors.

"Are you out of your mind?" I ask instantly.

She looks at me, wide-eyed. "What do you mean?"

"What are you doing here, Mia? I *live* here, you can't just be showing up like this," I say, a shiver running through my body as the wind cuts through me.

I watch as she crosses her arms in front of her. "Well, you said not to text you anymore."

"So you figured that meant show up unannounced at my apartment?" I ask incredulously.

Her nose tilts up. "You seem to have no trouble showing up at mine."

"That's because you aren't married with a child, Mia," I say, rubbing my forehead.

What a mess this is. I'm realizing now what a colossal mistake I've made. I rub my forehead and eyebrows hard enough to pull out a couple eyebrow hairs.

"Listen, I'm sorry about earlier, okay? It's just, your text last night, I didn't know what to make of it," I say finally.

Mia flicks up an eyebrow. "I thought it was pretty clear. I like you, Mark. That should be obvious by now."

I lick my lips. This is really starting to spiral. Even though I know where she's going with this, I still try and feign ignorance.

"And I like you too. But this..." I gesture between us, "can't interfere with this."

I point to the apartment building behind me. To my home. My *family's* home.

Mia remains silent, and I feel a need to fill the empty air as my pulse quickens.

"You're very important to me. Very important. I just... if I lose my family, I... I don't know if I'll want to see you very much, okay?"

Mia's eyes are harder than I've ever seen them when they meet mine. "Can't have it all, Mark."

I shake my head. "No, I can't. You're right about that. Just... just give me some time to figure this out, okay? To... to make some changes."

That seems to soften her up, and her demeanor relaxes.

"What, like divorce? You're saying you'll divorce Judith?" she asks.

My gut tightens as I realize that's what she thought I meant by *making changes*. Then again, I don't even know what I meant. I'm just saying words in the hope this will be over soon.

Against my better judgement, I give her a nod.

Mia smiles widely again and leans forward, apparently intending to kiss me. I stop it at the last second, holding her arms gently to keep her away from me.

"We'll talk soon, okay? I promise. Judith has a late night at work this week. I'll—I'll see you then."

Mia nods and winks at me. "Sounds like a plan, handsome. Looking forward to it."

And then she's headed off into the night, jeans

moving swiftly down the sidewalk. I stare after her for another moment, rubbing my hands together as I try to calm my heart rate and pull myself together.

Absolute nightmare. Somehow, everything seems to be falling apart at once.

No chance of breaking it off cleanly with Mia now. I've actually gone and told her I'll *divorce* Judith.

My stomach is in knots as I stagger back inside, my skin damp with sweat despite the cold. I dab at my forehead with the back of my hand and swallow.

Things are starting to come apart, and I'm not sure how long I can keep the pieces from crashing down around me.

Who'll be left standing when they eventually do?

TWELVE

JUDITH

I look up from my book as the front door swings open, and Mark steps back inside.

That took a lot longer than I expected.

"All good?" I ask.

He nods. Then my eyes drop to his hands, where there's no package in sight.

"What happened? You were gone a while," I say.

Mark licks his lips and nods again. "Yeah, I was trying to help the delivery guy. For some reason, he had our address, but it wasn't our names on the package."

He moves through the living room and into the kitchen, where I hear the fridge open.

I look back down at my book. It's plausible enough. And yet there's an odd, nagging feeling in my gut that just won't go away. I've had it all day, like a headache that just won't quit.

Still, I don't want to voice anything at this point. I know the power of words and how they change things.

When Mark comes back into the living room with a

glass of wine, I keep my head down, though I'm no longer reading. I notice he's only brought a glass for himself.

There isn't much noise beside the flipping of my page as I turn it.

Mark takes a sip. As inconspicuously as I can, I shift my eyes to the side and look him over, trying to decide if he's lying to me.

I've always struggled to read people accurately, given that I have a tendency to just expect disappointment and letdown from others.

Mother always said I was a Negative Nancy.

Is that what's happening here? Am I reading too much into things, letting my negative view of the world cloud my judgement?

If I'm not wrong, however...

Even just the thought is enough to send a cold shiver through me. Mark knows my stance on adultery.

I would like to trust my husband. And part of me does, I believe.

But then there's the other part of me, the part that has been let down by just about everyone I've ever known, over and over again.

My sister. My mother. My father.

That part of me has been trained not to take anything at face value.

I dislike it, and yet there it is.

So as Mark takes another large gulp from his wine glass and searches for the TV remote, I watch him.

I'm not entirely sure what I'm even looking for.

As far as I'm aware, he still cares for me. He does everything asked of him and rarely complains.

Whenever I ask if everything is fine, he will tell me that it is.

The television comes to life in front of us. Mark puts on a football game. I've never cared to watch, but I understand that he enjoys it. It allows him to focus on something simple and pure, as he's said in the past.

I wonder what he's trying to distract himself from now.

It could be the ongoing ordeal with my sister, sure. That's probably enough, given how much trouble she's been lately.

Sometimes I still wonder how he was ever married to her in the first place.

Settling back into my book, I work to try and just focus on the words, and not the thoughts strumming about in my brain. Mark remains glued to the television until the game is over, and then it's time for bed.

The next morning is business as usual. The alarm goes off in our bedroom, so Mark can get up and drop Amelia off at my sister's, and I can get to work. All of us work like a well-oiled machine, knowing our roles.

Amelia is in her room now, packing up her weekend bag for the trip. Mark is downstairs, feeding himself while I shower and get changed into something presentable. Once I've got my hair straightened, I come down the stairs to find Amelia and Mark ready to go.

I pop in a coffee pod as we chat a little. Everything feels normal. Maybe my suspicious thoughts from last night were misplaced.

When it's time to go, all of us head out of the apartment and walk to the elevator. They'll drop me off first at work and then drive over to Katie's to drop off Amelia, though Katie's place is closer than my office.

It's just better this way. Besides ensuring I get to work early—which is really on time—I have absolutely zero desire to so much as look at my sister.

Much better for Mark to be the middle-man.

The elevator doors ding open in the parking garage. As usual, I'm struck by the unpleasant odor of gasoline that seems perpetually trapped down here.

Mark has Amelia's weekend bag and backpack slung over his shoulder, the bags bouncing along his shoulder blades as he goes. A yawn escapes my mouth as I walk toward the car, the heels of my boots clacking against the paved floor.

I take a sip of my coffee to try and snap out of it—and then nearly spit it out as the car comes into view.

Mark stops walking, too. His voice cuts off mid-joke as both of us spot it.

"What?" Amelia asks, looking up in confusion and whipping her head between the two of us.

Mark licks his lips, his eyes sliding to me.

My jaw is set in a hard line, my pulse thudding. Once. Twice.

Not again.

Mark takes two more steps and then plucks a crumpled napkin that's been tucked neatly under the windshield wipers.

He unfolds it slowly. I watch as his eyes flick across the paper and then he crumples it up.

"Is that a note? What does it say Daddy?" Amelia asks, her voice full of interest.

Mark meets my gaze, and when he does, my entire body stiffens.

I can read his mind. It's happening again.

My head shakes as I purse my lips, feeling my blood move like ice through my veins.

All her promises. All her swearing up and down things would change.

Now here she is, leaving notes on the car again.

Judging from Mark's face, it's another nasty one, scrawled out in some drunken stupor.

This is exactly how it began the last time around. First it was notes. Then it was damage. Then it was real fear.

I don't care if she is my sister. Enough is enough. I gave her the benefit of the doubt with the beer can, but this confirms it.

Really, it's what I knew all along, only now I can tell Mark believes it too.

He's trying to dodge Amelia's many questions, loading stuff into the car while she only seems to grow more curious.

My mouth sets in a hard line as I pull out my phone. I will not allow my sister to play these games any longer. Once, and never again.

This time, she's going to find out that I can play back.

THIRTEEN
KATIE

I'm in the bathroom when I hear the knock at the door.

"Coming," I shout, hoping Mark can hear me.

I'm up this time, though not in the best condition. Knowing that, I've been in the bathroom applying some mascara and blush, trying to look more presentable to Mark and Amelia.

I give myself a final once-over in the mirror. Looking normal enough. I set down the make up and open up the bathroom door, chewing on a stick of gum. A nice mint flavor I was hoping would give me a little more pep in my step, but hasn't.

Just going to have to fake it, I suppose.

Trudging through the kitchen and living area, I suddenly become aware of how much takeout trash is scattered around. Empty styrofoam containers decorate the kitchen counter, coffee table, and even the couch.

So much for presentable. It's too late to do anything about it now. Mark's here with Amelia.

We'll go for a walk, breathe in some of this fresh fall air. I think that would do me good.

More knocking at the door.

"I said I'm coming," I shout, stubbing my toe against the wood foot of the couch in my hurry.

I swallow a curse and hobble up to the door, taking one last moment to draw a breath.

Remember, Mark mustn't suspect a thing.

With a big smile across my face, I unlock the door and pull it open.

"Good morning," I say, "how—"

Amelia's not with him. Why isn't she with him?

Mark stands alone in the doorway, a somber look on his face.

"What's wrong?" I ask, my heart thudding heavily in my chest.

"I've just come to tell you that we will be seeking full custody," he says.

The words rock me to my core. I blink, still trying to digest what he's telling me when he speaks again.

"Given everything... we just... we don't think you're fit to be Amelia's mother anymore, Katie. Not like this. I'm sorry."

I feel like my legs have just been chopped out from underneath me. The walls seem to swim behind Mark as I work to comprehend this.

"No longer... no longer fit? For my own child?" I ask, my voice rising in panic.

"Think of Amelia," Mark says. "Think of what's best for her."

I'm having trouble breathing. Full custody for them means I'll have no legal right to see my daughter.

Knowing the money Mark and Judith have at their disposal, coupled with my history, I have no doubt they'll be able to pull it off.

There's no amount of money Judith wouldn't spend to notch another victory on her belt. This would be the final victory, once and for all.

If only I hadn't gambled and drank away all my inheritance, I could use it to fight back.

But thanks to me and what I've done, I've got no money, no resources. It'll be a slaughter.

They're going to strip my daughter from me.

"Is this really the kind of environment you want our daughter to grow up in?" Mark asks sadly, gesturing behind me.

I do a half-turn, only barely seeing my place. It's dark, covered in trash.

Mark clears his throat. "The kind of... the kind of behaviors you want her exposed to?"

I whirl back around. The pointed accusation in his voice fills me with enough fire to retaliate.

"What behaviors, Mark? What behaviors?" I ask, taking a step forward.

Mark eases backward, eyes darting down the hallway. He must've seen someone, because he works to compose himself.

"You know exactly what behaviors, Katie. That's why I'm here," he says in a low voice.

How dare he accuse me of behaving improperly.

Accusing *me* when *he's* been the one to pry my daughter away from me, turn her against me.

I see now what he's been planning all along. The long con.

All those promises of co-parenting. Shared custody.

Now here we are, and the truth is laid bare. He wants to steal my daughter from me.

The walls quiver as I lower myself to the couch arm. Everything seems slightly blurry. This isn't real. This can't be happening.

As if looking through the wrong end of a telescope, I see him take a step forward, coming right up to the door-frame again.

"I'm sorry, but you've left us no other choice," Mark says quietly.

"Our lawyers will contact you soon," he finishes, and then he's gone.

He's left the door open. Leaving me alone. Utterly and completely alone.

I try to get air into my lungs, but it's impossible. It's like every atom of oxygen has been removed from the environment. I slide off the couch arm and hit the floor as the first sob escapes me.

It sounds like a strangled animal, not even human. *I can't lose my daughter.*

She is all I have left. There is nothing else in my life but her. The only thing that matters, and he wants to take that from me.

As I lie there, back against the ratty leather of my couch, world spiraling down, something shifts inside me.

It's a thought that changes things. Moves me from a

desperate sadness to a calm finality. The life-raft-in-a-swirling-ocean feeling begins to subside, and I sit up a little straighter.

A cold chill runs down my spine as the thought expands, multiplying itself in my mind. I sniff, wiping at my nose.

The answer. My response to Mark's attempt to destroy me.

If I can't see my daughter, then maybe he shouldn't be allowed to either. Ever, ever again.

FOURTEEN
MARK

There is nothing but dread.

It's the only emotion I feel as I walk into Central Park, my hands stuffed into my pockets.

All around me, people chatter away happily as they walk to and fro. I feel more like a man heading for the gallows.

It's time to fully talk things through with Mia.

I don't know how this is going to go. I don't even know how I *want* this to go.

All of last night, I laid awake in bed thinking over what I could possibly say to her. I can't divorce Judith, I just can't.

Knowing her, she'll crush me. She'll use anything and everything I've ever done, said or even thought to make sure I don't get Amelia.

And that's who I really care about. Judith will weaponize my daughter against me, I have zero doubt about that. Winning is all that matters for her.

And she always wins. I've seen that firsthand more times than anyone.

So really, there is no possible positive outcome of today's talk with Mia.

I chose the park instead of her place, so I can leave when it's over. A public setting will hopefully prevent any sort of incident from occurring as well. Hopefully.

I push out a heavy lungful of air and suck in the cold as I move further into the park. Horses clop along beside me. People on bikes shoot past, moving almost faster than I can see them.

I wish I was on a bike, speeding away to somewhere far from here.

Definitely a fall-weather day today. Even with the sun, the air bites at my skin.

My fingers find the zipper of my puffer vest and pull it up all the way to cover my neck a little better. The sound of my shoes against the sidewalk fills my ears as I go.

Every step takes me closer to a conversation I absolutely do not want to have.

No matter which way it goes, I lose something. Either way, a woman will hate me, and either of them could totally wreck my life, just in different ways. Not good.

A dog pulls at its leash to try and sniff me, the owner apologizing as I scoot past. I'm only a couple minutes' walk away now. There's no more putting it off.

I don't know how long this is going to take, either. Thankfully Judith had to work again today.

After delivering the news to Katie, I took Amelia to my Mom's for a little playdate. She loves Gammie.

Probably because Mom spoils Amelia rotten, even though she really doesn't have the money to, given she's a retired phlebotomist living off Social Security and whatever money I can convince her to take from me.

But at least some members of this family are having fun today.

It's now a little after four PM. After I'm done here, I'll pick up Amelia from Mom's and head back home, arriving well before Judith gets back from work.

Slipping my hands from my pockets, I rub them together and then blow on them. Maybe the chilly weather will actually work in my favor.

Mia isn't a huge fan of the cold, which means she probably won't want to be out for very long. I step off the pavement and start trekking across the grass now, closing in on my final destination.

It's this massive tree we had a picnic under last summer. I don't see Mia yet, which is more of a relief than I care to admit.

Not like I'll be able to relax for long, though. She's coming soon enough, and it'd be foolish to think otherwise.

I come to a stop at the tree and take a look around. A few people sit on blankets in the field around me, enjoying the sun while they still can. A check of my watch shows 4:09.

We were supposed to meet here at four. A little spark of hope lights in my chest, even as I try and stop it. Wild thoughts begin to spin.

What if she decided not to show?

What if she's tired of the whole married-man thing and done with me altogether?

And then I see her, and those stupid, desperate hopes are squashed.

She's walking quickly across the grass, a scarf wrapped around her neck and hands stuffed into her jacket pockets. Upon seeing me, she perks up noticeably.

That makes my heart sink even lower. This is going to be absolutely brutal.

Nothing to be done now but face my doom head-on. I raise a hand and wave, managing to prop a smile on my face despite the inner dread I feel.

"Sorry I'm late," Mia says as she comes up to me, pulling me into a hug with a kiss. "You know how the subways are on weekends."

I didn't think I could feel any guiltier, but as our lips connect, somehow I do. I break off the kiss and then rub my hands together.

"Good to see you, good to see you," I say.

I'm stalling. Trying to put off what I know has to be said.

"Sorry about coming by last night uninvited. Thinking back on it, that was a little crazy," Mia says with a small laugh.

Letting out a breath, I steel myself. Here we go—no more putting it off any longer.

"Listen," I say, "there's something I need to tell you."

Mia's pretty eyes fix on me with interest. I've got her attention. All I need to do now is tell her in plain English that we can't see each other anymore, as gently as I can.

Her eyes really are beautiful. I can tell by the way

she's looking at me how much she cares for me. I run my tongue over my lips to wet them.

"I... spoke with a lawyer."

The words rush out of me before I've even really grasped them. Mia's eyes widen.

"About divorcing Judith?" she asks.

What in the world am I doing? Stop it, Mark—stop right now.

"Uh-huh," I say, managing a small smile.

Mia pulls me into a hug with a squeal of excitement. I hardly react, still trying to figure out why those words came out of my mouth.

I was going to tell her we were done. That's what I came here to do.

Now she's thanking me and telling me how exciting this is, how much she already loves Amelia. I think I'm nodding, but I'm not entirely sure.

Mia pushes herself up onto her toes to kiss me again.

"For a moment I was a little concerned," she says with another laugh.

Another chance. *Tell her, Mark. Say it. Please.*

"No need for that," I say with a grin of my own.

I hate myself.

Mia reaches into her tote bag for a blanket, a large fuzzy one that we spread out atop the grass. Out next comes a thermos, filled with spiked hot chocolate. The warm liquid does nothing to quell the cold realization that has settled upon me.

I can't do what needs to be done. Instead, I simply pushed back the conversation.

Who knows how long this has bought me? At least no one is disappointed or angry at me, for now.

Undoubtedly, someone will be in the future. But not right now, and I guess that's what matters.

Taking another sip of the chocolate, I try to focus on the conversation with Mia. We chat about nothing serious, keeping it light. Somehow, I even come off as witty, Mia throwing back her head in laughter more than once.

Soon enough I'm going to have to head back to Mom's so I can pick up Amelia before Judith gets home.

Halfway through her next sentence, Mia stops talking and grins again.

"I'm sorry—I just need to hug you again."

She leans forward and grips me tight.

"Thanks for being so wonderful," she says, her voice slightly muffled by my puffer vest.

There's a strange feeling in my chest as she holds me.

It's a knowing about myself, as if some final piece of my character has finally been revealed.

I am a weak, weak man.

FIFTEEN

JUDITH

I didn't go to work today. I only told Mark I did.

Sitting here now, watching my husband kiss his daughter's schoolteacher in broad daylight in Central Park, I almost wish I had just gone to work.

Then I wouldn't have known anything.

Then I would not have to do something about it.

I continue to stare, my breathing coming in short, raspy gasps as my vision remains locked on the two of them. They've just shared a final goodbye kiss and are now headed in separate directions.

I was right. My gut instinct was right.

To think I started off today actually feeling slightly guilty for lying to Mark about having work. Given that it's Saturday, and most Saturdays I end up having to go in, he didn't even blink an eye.

The look on his face as he left Katie's place was nearly enough to make me forget the whole thing altogether.

But then he dropped Amelia off at his mother's, without ever having mentioned he was going to do that. And *then* he left his mother's. Alone.

With my bulky coat, scarf, and beanie on, I'm basically unrecognizable. So it was easy to follow him, walking far enough behind that he didn't suspect a thing.

Following him down into the subway was a much bigger risk. Just thinking of the filth was enough to make me shiver. Still, I had to know.

So somehow I found it inside me to step down those steps and descend into the cesspool, nose upturned as I darted my eyes around for my husband. I nearly missed the train he'd stepped into, barely managing to slip inside the subway car on the opposite end before the doors shut.

Having so many people packed in around me was nauseating. Couple that with the fact my husband was less than twenty feet away, unaware I was stalking him, and it's a wonder I held onto my breakfast.

More than once I considered what I could possibly say in explanation if I was caught, but it didn't happen.

His head never came up from his phone. That handsome, lying, cheating head.

Then we were walking into the park, me trailing him about a hundred feet back.

Mark was moving with purpose, clearly with a destination in mind. I was working hard to try and keep pace with him, which left little time for my brain to try and figure out where he was going or who he might be seeing.

And then he stopped. Underneath a massive tree, its leaves a cheerful red and orange bouquet overhead. I moved to a bench out of his line of sight and sat down, still feeling like I must be wrong about all this.

That maybe this was just some impromptu guy meet-up, a chance to throw a football around or something.

And then I saw her. Ms. Mia, as Amelia calls her. The teacher.

Of course it's the teacher.

Suddenly it became crystal clear why Mark always volunteers for pick-up and drop-off. It isn't solely because of his desire to spend more time with his daughter.

There was someone else he wanted to see, too.

I feel my skin warming beneath my clothes as my gaze follows Mark. He's trudging away from the field with his hands buried in his jean pockets. Head down, looking at his shoes.

Oblivious to the fact that his wife is now aware of his infidelity.

It hits me that he has purposefully, willingly, actively destroyed our perfect life together.

I don't know how long this has been going on, but then again, I suppose it doesn't really matter, does it?

What matters is that it *is* going on. He has betrayed me, sabotaged us. My mind races as I sit there.

He thinks he's winning right now, I bet. "Getting one over" on me, as it were.

The man thinks he can make a fool of me. My jaw sets in a hard line. I will not stand for it.

The humiliation of having to delete our shared social media photos. The pestering questions from colleagues about the disappearance of my ring.

The sheer shame of having to explain that my husband had eyes for another woman. That apparently, I was not enough for him.

I swallow as Mark moves out of sight in the distance. Behind him, the sky loses light by the second. My body remains rooted to the park bench.

This filthy bench, probably sat upon by thousands before me. Right now, the thought hardly even bothers me.

I'm too focused on how to destroy my worthless rat of a husband.

My brain surges with ideas, but none of them feel adequate. Nothing rises to the level of his act of betrayal against me.

And there must be total victory, otherwise there's no point in even trying.

I cannot tolerate cheating. I cannot stand by while my husband splatters mud all over the pristine painting that was my life.

Up until now, my reality was perfect. All my hard work had finally paid off, and I'd gotten everything I'd ever dreamed about.

A high-powered, well-respected job. The perfect husband. A darling adopted daughter. A beautiful home in the most prestigious city in this country.

Now it appears that was all an illusion. My life was never perfect to begin with.

When I rise from the bench, I'm trembling enough that I have trouble pulling my phone from my pocket.

Mark expects me home soon. I cannot wait to hear the lie he will feed me when I ask him about his day.

My footsteps are even, controlled, moving me through the dusk. My gaze stays up, locked on the park's exit in front of me.

It has become clear to me that if I'm ever to feel successful and complete, there is more hard work yet to come.

SIXTEEN
KATIE

I stare at the bottle on my countertop.

I don't remember buying it. And yet somehow, here it is in my apartment. Just sitting there on the counter, glistening in the dying sunlight.

A promise. A seduction.

The room is dark around me. I don't want the lights on. I don't want to see what I look like.

Days have passed in a stupor. It might be Tuesday or Wednesday, I don't know. I don't care.

Not showing up to work on the weekend got me fired, I think. At least that's what the voicemail from my boss made it sound like. Oh well.

The apartment has a strange smell from the trash that has yet to be cleaned up. A normal person would just take it out, maybe crack a window.

But I am not normal. My husband and my sister have just announced they will be taking my child from me, permanently.

The papers arrived just as Mark said they would. Sheets and sheets filled with legal jargon. The summary?

Amelia will be ours. Your own flesh and blood will no longer belong to you.

The papers are somewhere behind me, scattered around. Crumpled and torn. My eyes drift to the bottle of vodka on the counter in front of me. Its liquid is clear, pristine.

When I drink, I black out. When I black out, I do bad things. Have done them in the past.

Part of the reason Mark and I separated in the first place.

But even quitting drinking hard liquor for years wasn't enough for him. Nothing ever would've been, as *this* was his plan all along.

The longer I stare at the bottle, the more I wonder what the point is.

What has sobriety gotten me?

No matter what, I'll always be the black sheep of the family. The shameful daughter of the high-powered business executive, nothing like her wonderful, successful sister.

My bleary eyes peer around in the darkness at the terrible apartment I'm forced to live in.

This is my life. Spent in the darkness, now that the one shining light is being stripped away.

Nothing I do will change that, so what's the point?

The vodka grows in my vision as I step closer, licking my lips. There's an ache in my chest like I've never felt before. Powerful like a magnet as I'm pulled forward.

What's the point?

Amelia is no longer mine. My life is no longer mine. With a shaking hand, I reach over and grab hold of the cap.

The bottle is cool beneath my warm palm. That makes the ache even stronger.

My life is over anyway. With that being the case, I might as well enjoy myself. I've fought for long enough. Forced myself to conform to what others expected of me.

Look where that got me.

A loud crack echoes through the space around me as I break the seal and twist off the cap. It rolls off the counter and bounces to the floor to spin off somewhere behind me.

The sharp scent of the alcohol hits my nose, and the last of my resistance falls away. The promise screams itself in my mind, and now, I'm done fighting it.

Yes, bad things happen when I drink, but then again, I have absolutely nothing more to lose.

Mark has seen to that.

SEVENTEEN

MARK

I don't realize Judith is right behind me until I turn around.

"Woah," I say, nearly dropping the glass of water I just filled from the fridge tap.

My jerk of surprise makes some of the water spill over the lip of the glass and splash onto the floor.

Pulling a sheet of paper towel off the roll, I squat down to dab it up.

"Scared me," I say with a little chuckle.

Judith doesn't smile.

"Sorry," she says after a few seconds.

I watch her as she moves to the cupboard and pulls it open. She pulls out a coffee pod and places it into the coffee machine. The movement seems even more mechanical than usual.

"Everything okay?" I ask as I straighten back up.

Judith glances over at me and nods. "Fine. Just still waking up."

I look her over for another second before she turns

away, her back to me. A small lump forms in my throat as a voice in my head whispers.

Maybe she knows.

Before I really let it take root, I shake it off. She can't know. I've been careful enough, haven't I?

It's probably just because of the early hour. Usually she remains in bed while I get up to take Amelia to school, but not today, I guess.

I think about saying something else to her but decide against it. If she's crabby, it's best to just leave her be. Instead, I head back into the living room to peer up the spiral staircase to the second floor.

"Almost ready, Cap'n?" I shout up.

"Coming Dad," Amelia says.

Then she appears at the glass balustrade, uniform sweater on with the shirt underneath not tucked in. I clap my hands as she bounds down the stairs.

"Go–go–go," I say.

She races by me into the kitchen, where I've already prepared her breakfast. We'll head out in another ten or fifteen minutes.

Judith greets Amelia and then strides out of the kitchen and into the living room.

"Up a little earlier today, huh?" I say to her.

Judith nods but doesn't reply. Hmm.

That makes my pulse quicken ever-so-slightly, though I work hard not to let it show. As casually as I can, I move to pick up the TV remote and click the power button while glancing at her out of the corner of my eye.

Does she suspect something?

Judith isn't even looking at me right now, instead

gazing out the windows to her left that let in the early morning glow. At this hour, the city is nearly stagnant, but it won't stay that way for much longer.

I chew my lip as I direct my attention away from her and onto the TV again. I really hope we do exchange a few words this morning, just enough to tell me that everything is alright.

Especially today, I don't need anything else to think about.

Today is the anniversary of my dad's death. I want today to be thinking only about him, to honor him. It's hard enough to remember him as is, given how few memories I have of him.

Even the ones I do have feel more like pictures in my mind, just flashes of his face smiling at me as he held me. The last thing I need is even more thoughts piled on top and crowding those fragile remnants out.

Judith glances down at her phone and then stirs.

"Oh my—today is your dad, right?" she asks.

I nod. "Yeah. I already called off work. I'm headed to the park after I drop Amelia off so I can do my thing."

Judith pushes up off the couch and walks over to me, pulling me into a hug.

"Of course. Take the time you need. I think it's wonderful you honor him," she says.

I soften into her embrace, relief flooding through me. We're good. All that earlier worry was just my guilty conscience eating away at me.

And it really is eating away.

Looking in the mirror this morning, I hardly recognized myself. My face appeared almost gaunt, with purple circles beneath my eyes from the lack of restful sleep. Like my secrets are draining the life out of me.

What other choice do I have, though? I couldn't tell Mia the truth, I just couldn't.

She was looking at me with such care and admiration. To crush that would've been too much to bear. I couldn't stand to see those big eyes move from love to hate.

Not yet. I don't want to be the bad guy just yet.

Judith and I separate as she glances down at her phone again. "Ought to get moving, don't you think? Chance of rain today—means there might be more cars on the road."

I nod. Back to our regularly scheduled programming.

"Okay baby girl, chop-chop," I say as we head into the kitchen where Amelia's been eating her breakfast.

She pushes her bowl of whole-wheat cereal away from her and reaches for the glass of sugar free orange juice beside her hand. She drains it and then slides off the chair.

"Where's your backpack?" I ask her.

She thinks for a moment. "Still upstairs. I'll get it."

She takes off again, leaving Judith and me alone in the kitchen. As I turn to her, I find her looking at me.

"What?" I ask.

"I just know how much your parents mean to you. Are you sure you don't want me to take Amelia to school today?" she asks.

I blink. The offer takes me by surprise. My mind moves quickly. If I say no, she'll probably wonder why I'm insisting. Especially today, when there's simply no good reason for me to be the one to drop Amelia off.

Besides, it might actually be good to avoid seeing Mia today. So I look back at Judith with a smile.

"That would actually be wonderful. Thank you," I say.

It'll give me more time at the park with Dad. So when Amelia shoots back down the stairs, backpack in hand, we let her know Judith will be driving today.

"Why?" Amelia asks.

"Today is Daddy's day to think about Grandpa," I say.

Amelia nods solemnly. Obviously we've never shared the whole story with her, but she is aware that my dad is no longer with us.

"Okay. I'm sorry Daddy," she says sweetly, stepping forward to hug me.

She's so little that she only comes up to my hip. I hold her, feeling my chest tighten.

"Thank you, sweetheart. Now get moving before you're late," I say.

Amelia opens the front door as I look back at Judith.

"Thanks again," I say.

She smiles. "That's what married couples do isn't it? Be there for each other?"

Then she's moving past me. The door is pulled shut, and I'm left in the kitchen alone, my glass of water beside me.

Something about that sentence doesn't sit exactly right with me, sticking in my mind for a moment as I listen to the two of them head for the elevator. It dings open, and I shake myself out of it.

Time to use the extra time and head for Central Park.

With nothing else to do today, my mind is allowed to think freely and focus on Dad.

He occupies my thoughts as I take the train up. I've got my headphones in, playing a soundtrack made up of his favorite songs. Or at least, the songs Mom told me were his favorites. I was barely two years old when he died.

The train is packed as usual, given the time of the day. At my stop, I squeeze out of the car and start up the stairs to the surface. I know exactly where I'm headed. I could probably walk there blindfolded, if I had to.

Dad's bench. Many of the benches in the park have been dedicated to someone, the honor denoted by a small, engraved plaque affixed to the back. After Dad passed, Mom had one of them dedicated in his honor.

For me, it's become like a headstone. A place I can go to be with him.

It's located in The Bramble, a hilly, heavily-wooded section of the park that feels more like you're upstate rather than in the center of NYC.

I've always loved the seclusion of it. Most of the time, I'm completely alone, any street noise swallowed up by the dense foliage.

Before entering the park, I grab a coffee and sip it while looking across the street at the edge of the park. The wall of trees looks almost surreal when paired with the skyscrapers around me.

It's a nice moment, just sitting there, headphones in. My own little world, where nothing and no one can find me. Just me and Dad. The world rushes on around me, moving to and fro as everyone hurries to their places of work.

Once the coffee is finished, I exit the coffee shop and start across the street and into the park. Cars honk from somewhere behind me.

Moving into the park is a good stretch of my legs, now that I have open sidewalk in front of me. I maximize it, walking quickly in time with the music.

It takes maybe fifteen minutes or so to make my way up to the entrance to The Bramble. I walk across a small, ornate bridge, stopping at the center to peer down at the water and the pair of swans that float by. Buildings rise up from behind the trees in front of me.

How simple a swan's existence is. Apparently they mate for life. That makes my stomach twinge, and I look away.

Today is about Dad, nothing else.

As I push away from the bridge's railing, I get a strange feeling. Almost like someone is staring at me or something. Looking around though, I can't spot anyone who seems to be paying any attention to me.

After another moment, I shrug it off and finish walking across the bridge to enter into The Bramble section of the park.

The elevation increases instantly here, trees and bushes replacing the grass. Birds and squirrels dash through the underbrush as I walk past. Completely oblivious to me.

I pass a couple of morning-walkers on my way in, nodding politely to them as we move by each other. It takes another few minutes of hiking before I arrive at Dad's bench. It's situated on a small offshoot path.

"Hey Dad," I say under my breath as I reach out a hand and touch the plaque.

Sitting down, I soon find myself lost in deep thought. The forest seems to grow in around me, every inch of my vision filled with shades of green and brown. My breath forms a small cloud as I push it out, watching it move upwards before fading.

A squirrel skitters across the gravel in front of me, pausing to gaze at me for a moment before deciding I'm not going to give him any food. He bounds off into the leaves again. I watch him go.

Apparently Mom and Dad used to come up here and sit together when they first started dating. This was their favorite section of the park.

Once they got married, they still came here and shared lunch. Life hadn't been easy, but they'd found each other, and they'd stuck together.

When Dad got the big promotion, this was where they celebrated. Two young people and then a family of three, the whole world ahead of them.

Then Dad got fired, right when things were looking up. After searching for months and finding nothing, he took another way out.

As much as I want to think exclusively about Dad, I find my thoughts returning to the last thing Judith said to me. About how couples are there for each other.

It seemed slightly odd in the moment, and even weirder now. My stomach twinges.

What if she *is* onto me? Just the idea of that is enough

to make my palms break into a sweat, despite the cool temperature of the morning air.

The more I think about it, the more certain I am. Judith is not one to spout off sentences like that.

No, if she spoke it, then it had meaning. I swallow hard, feeling flighty.

Another thought moves through my head, picking up steam until it forges to the front of my mind, bringing with it a profound sense of dread.

Katie is mad at me already. Probably hates me with every fiber of her being. If Judith knows the truth, then she feels the same way.

Both of them might even want me dead.

I shift uncomfortably on the bench, suddenly aware of just how secluded this section of the park is. Forest in every direction.

Katie is a loose cannon. Even more so if she's really started drinking again. Liable to do just about anything.

Judith on the other hand, is cold and calculating. She never says a word out of turn. Everything with her is methodical, planned, particular.

It dawns on me that of all the mistakes I've made in my life—and I've made some serious ones—causing both of the Rose sisters to hate me might be the biggest.

It might just be the death of me.

Then I hear a branch snap behind me and realize I've understood that a little too late.

PART 2

EIGHTEEN

KATIE

I wake up on the floor, covered in blood.

My head snaps up with a gasp, the pulsing in my temples so strong it's hard to keep my eyes open. A searing pain flashes across my leg—my knee is cut open.

Even just trying to sit up makes me gag with pain. My arm feels weird, bruised. Maybe from sleeping at a weird angle on a wood floor.

Either way, I'm not feeling so hot.

Blinking, I slowly push myself up to a seated position with my legs out in front of me, panting slightly.

The headache is almost overpowering. I want to just shut my eyes and disappear from existence right now. My stomach is tight. Nausea washes over me as I lift my head and look around.

I'm in my apartment, on the floor. Only I've got my shoes on. I never wear my shoes inside, which means I must've left.

That's when it hits me—I have absolutely no recollection of how I got here.

Glancing down at my shirt reveals more spots of blood in addition to the cut on my knee that I have zero memory of opening.

That freaks me out even more than the blood. It's one thing to hurt yourself, quite another to realize you have no idea how you did it.

My heart pounds against my ribs as I push up against the couch, wincing and licking my lips. I'm trying to piece things together.

What's the last thing I remember?

The bottle on the counter. My aching eyes dart over to the countertop, but the bottle of vodka is gone. I remember cracking the seal, smelling the sharp bite of the alcohol, and then...

Blank. I swallow hard.

I drank so much I blacked out again. Blacked out and then apparently *went* out, judging by my shoes. Unbelievable.

Guilt wracks my body, causing an ache that competes with every other thing I'm feeling right now. It takes effort, but I get myself up onto the couch. I need to take a breather afterward, my head is spinning so hard.

I haven't had a hangover like this in years. Then again, I haven't had hard liquor in years. Looks like my tolerance has dropped way off.

It's like every inch of my body is in some sort of painful or sore state at this point. My throat feels so dry it actually hurts to swallow. What I should do is just walk over to the sink and get some water, but that feels like an impossible task right now.

All I can do is remain slouched on the couch and try

to dig through my exhausted brain for any memories of the past day.

Even focusing with my eyes shut, all I keep coming back to is the bottle of vodka. Then it's like a wall of darkness.

Whatever happened after the bottle opened, I quite literally have no memory of it. That makes my skin prickle.

If I left the apartment, where did I go?

And how did I cut myself? My attention moves to my knee, the pain of which has slowly overtaken everything else.

It's a pretty deep gash. The torn fabric of my jeans is darkened from the blood, making it stiff. Reaching forward, I gingerly try to pull away the ripped fabric from the edges of the wound without disturbing it and let out a hiss.

Some of the denim material has dried onto the wound. I hobble to the drawer and open it in search of my boxcutter to slice the jeans off my leg. They're already ruined anyway.

I can't find it, which means I'll have to take them off the usual way.

That's when I get a look at my fingernails in the light from the kitchen window. They're absolutely filthy. Blinking to try and see more clearly, I hold both hands up to my face.

There's a solid layer of black dirt absolutely caked underneath my nails. Picking at it dislodges some of it, the small bits landing on my lap.

What did I do last night?

I just wish there was something, anything that I could remember. I look around for my phone, but don't see it. That makes my stomach pang again.

If I lost it somewhere, I'm in big trouble. There's simply no way I can afford to buy a new one right now.

It takes almost everything I have, but I manage to push off the couch arm and up to a standing position.

My back is hunched forward from the horrible sleeping position. Everything is tight and achy as I stagger toward the kitchen counter.

Pouring a cold glass of water and chugging it helps a little, wetting down the layers of cotton that seem to be stuffed into my brain. After I've consumed the entire glass, I turn right around and pour myself another one.

I feel like a mummy having life breathed back into me. It takes three glasses before I feel human enough to try and locate my phone.

I'm working hard not to absolutely freak out here. No phone, covered in blood and dirt. Obviously, I got into some sort of mess last night. As usual.

With guilt and regret beating my brow in equal measure, I push away from the counter with a grunt.

Please let it be in here somewhere.

Staggering over to the light switch, I flick it on. There were only a couple lamps on before, but now the entire apartment is flooded with light.

As such, I'm able to spot my phone atop the sheets of my bed, still plugged into the charger. Relief rushes through me as I make my way over to it.

Thank goodness. I do remember plugging it in before

spotting the vodka bottle yesterday, which means I didn't even take it with me whenever I went.

Extremely dangerous behavior. Beads of sweat form at my brow as I think about how vulnerable I was last night.

No phone, no memory. Anything could've happened to me.

I land hard on the bed, the mattress bouncing me up a little before settling. My stiff fingers grope for my phone. When the screen lights up, I nearly have a heart attack.

It's four in the afternoon. The next day. I'm missing almost twenty-four hours from my memory.

Even though the brightness makes my head scream, I open up my phone.

There are no messages, which is both good and bad. No one texting me, telling me about everything I did wrong last night.

On the other hand, I still have zero clue about where I could've gone. Since I didn't bring my phone with me, that means zero new pictures in my camera roll, either.

Nothing to help me piece together the night.

And then I move over to calls, and suck in a breath. I called Mark fifteen times in a row yesterday. No memory of that whatsoever.

All of the calls took place before five P.M..

Looks like he didn't pick up once or even try to call me back. I drop the phone and rub my face.

I can't believe I called him that many times. What a mess.

At this point though, that's the least of my concerns.

He is trying to take away my daughter. Guess I really wanted to talk to him last night about that.

My stomach rolls over again at the thought. That is followed shortly by another rolling wave of anger.

I'm actually grateful for it, because it helps mitigate some of the agony I'm otherwise steeping in.

I almost want to call him another fifteen times. Let him really have it.

Then the wave of nausea comes over me again, and I'm up and rushing to the bathroom. For the next few minutes, there's nothing but the pounding in my head to focus on as I vomit into the toilet.

As I empty into the bowl, the urge to talk with Mark leaves, too. I think we're past that point now.

As far as I'm concerned, Mark is dead to me.

NINETEEN
JUDITH

I wait until the morning to file the missing person's report.

Perhaps I shouldn't have waited that long, but I did. This is my first time experiencing something like this, after all.

Amelia is upstairs getting ready for school, oblivious to everything as I wait on hold with the police.

"New York City Police Department Missing Persons Unit, this is Officer Richards," a woman says over the phone.

"Yes, I'd like to report a missing person," I say.

"Okay, Ma'am. Who do you think is missing?"

"My husband, Mark Wharton. He didn't come last night before I went to bed. I just got up this morning, and there's still no sign of him," I say.

It might sound slightly grotesque to admit, but I've always wondered how I'd react in a situation like this. If I'd still be able to think clearly and logically.

Apparently some people can hardly function in a

crisis, and I couldn't help but wonder if maybe, despite my other traits, I was one of those people.

Now I have my answer. I flick my eyes to the clock on the stove. If we want to get Amelia to school on time, this is going to have to move quickly.

"Okay, and your husband... when was the last time you saw him?" the woman asks after typing something out.

"Yesterday morning, before I dropped his daughter off at school. He told me he was headed to Central Park," I reply.

"And you expected him to return home yesterday at what time?" the woman asks.

I take a second to think about an answer. "I'm not sure if there was an expected time, actually. He had taken the day off of work, which makes me think he planned to be out quite a while. At the very least, I would've expected him home by dinner. If not, he would've texted me otherwise."

More clicking as the woman makes more notes. "Okay..." she says.

"And he left about what time?"

"I left the house before he did, so I'm not sure about that. I'd guess some time around eight AM," I say.

There are more questions asked, which I answer to the best of my ability. They want to know Mark's age, date of birth, appearance. They ask what he was last seen wearing, and if he has any history of mental health issues.

Then they ask about his recent behavior.

"Any unusual actions or circumstances in the days leading up to his disappearance?" the officer asks.

I swallow to buy myself some time. Should I mention the cheating?

If I do, they might assume *I* had something to do with Mark's disappearance. It certainly wouldn't be too far of a stretch to make.

Instead, I shake my head. "Not that I can recall. He seemed normal to me."

The officer then informs me that a detective will be coming by to further assist on the case.

Amelia comes bounding down the staircase, backpack bouncing up and down before she reaches the bottom.

"Where's Daddy?" she asks, looking around the kitchen.

I quickly try and determine what to share with her. "Daddy is... he's out right now, okay? So I'm going to take you to school again."

Amelia nods and steps up to her chair against the kitchen island. I look down at the marble countertop in front of her, suddenly realizing there's no cereal for her to eat. I quickly get breakfast made, and then we're out the door.

The sky overhead is gloomy, grey clouds hanging low over the city. They seem to press down toward me as I drop Amelia off. I don't wait around but speed back home so I can be there in plenty of time before the detective arrives.

Back inside, I stand in front of my closet trying to decide what I should wear. It's important I appear worried, and a worried wife probably wouldn't be looking her absolute best. For that reason, I decided not to straighten my hair this morning.

I'm downstairs making coffee when the wall phone rings with a call from the front desk. A police detective is here to see me. I tell them to send him up.

There's a bit of moisture on my palms, so I smooth them across the sides of my shirt. I'm usually not one for nerves, but today is different.

This has to go exactly how I saw it playing out in my mind.

A soft knock at the door brings my head up. I move across the length of the apartment and then pull open the door.

The detective stands in the hallway wearing a suit, though it's not the right size. The sleeves hang too far down on his hands, even when he raises one to shake mine.

"Mrs. Wharton? I'm Detective Scalini," he says.

I resist the urge to correct him on my last name. It's Rose-Wharton, but now is absolutely not the time to vocalize that.

"Please, come in," I say. "Thank you for coming over."

Detective Scalini steps inside with a cough.

"Beautiful home," he says with a nod.

I give him a tight-lipped smile. "Thank you."

"So I know you spoke with an officer over the phone, but I'd just like to ask you some questions as well, if you wouldn't mind," Scalini says.

He then proceeds to ask me many of the same questions I've already answered.

"And the last time you saw Mark was yesterday morning, correct? At around eight AM?"

"Yes, that's right. I saw him right before Amelia and I left to drop her off at school," I say.

"And has your husband ever done anything like this before?" he asks.

"Taken off without alerting you, I mean."

I shake my head. "Not that I can remember, no. He wouldn't just leave, officer. His daughter Amelia, she lives with us."

Scalini nods and scribbles something down into his notebook. Then he looks up.

"And you told the officer over the phone that everything had seemed normal with Mark, correct?" he asks.

I nod, careful not to reveal anything with my facial expressions. There's no doubt they'll find out about the infidelity, but it's important for me to seem like I had no idea, thereby eliminating me as any sort of suspect in Mark's disappearance, given I'd have no plausible reason.

The detective writes something else down. "Okay, Mrs. Wharton, thank you for your time."

He starts to get up.

"What happens next? I mean, what am I supposed to do? What do I tell Amelia?" I ask.

Scalini thinks it over for a moment, then sits back down. "Listen, I just want to be completely honest with you here. From what I can gather, right now I'm leaning toward the belief that Mark might've just... decided he doesn't want to be here, for whatever reason."

"See, as an adult, Mark doesn't legally need to come

home," Scalini continues. "We've certainly seen it before."

I shake my head. "But his daughter. He wouldn't leave her."

Scalini looks down but says nothing. After another moment, he checks his phone.

"If that's everything, I'll be going now," he says, glancing at me.

I nod, swallowing. Scalini nods in return and then stands, buttoning his suit.

"Thank you for your time, Mrs. Wharton. I'll be sure to let you know if we have any news."

I walk the detective to the door, offering him thanks for his help. After he leaves, I watch him walk down the hallway for a moment before closing the door. Only after I shut it, do I allow myself to fully breathe out.

My hands are trembling, ever-so-slightly. I rub my palms on my shirt again.

Thankfully, Detective Scalini didn't seem to notice or care. Maybe he assumed they were trembling from worry.

I however, know the real reason.

They were trembling because I was not wholly truthful with a police officer.

TWENTY
KATIE

This is the hangover to rule all hangovers.

Today is day two, and still my head aches. I spent yesterday doing little more than lying on the couch, as every movement felt like it might cause me to vomit profusely.

While the headache persists, at least the nausea has finally subsided today. That means I can at least try to become a functioning human being again.

Without the pain taking precedence, I'm left with nothing to distract from the onslaught of thoughts pounding through my skull.

Mark still hasn't called me back. Not even a text, which makes me all the more nervous.

What if I went over there when I was black-out drunk? What if I did something?

The thought gives me chills as I stand over the sink, eyes shut tight. I pour myself a glass of tap water and drink it down. I'm sure I'm just overreacting.

If I did do something, I'd probably be looking at a long message from Mark, not radio silence.

That makes me feel a little better, until another thought rises to the surface.

Unless I did something really, *really* bad.

I think back to the pulsing anger I felt toward him in the hours before I started drinking. I blamed him for everything that had happened to me.

A coil of worry tightens in my stomach. We already know I'm an angry drunk. That coupled with all the emotions I was feeling that afternoon...

A shaky breath pours out of me. All of this is just the post-alcohol anxiety talking. It has to be.

Shuffling to the fridge, I pull it open in search of something to eat.

Now that the upset stomach has gone away, I'm absolutely starving. There's nothing but some days-old Thai food in a styrofoam box. It'll have to do.

Grabbing the noodle box in one hand, I pull out my phone with the other.

Still no messages. No one telling me how horrible I was.

That might be the strangest part of all of this. Every time I've blacked out in the past, I felt like I was holding my breath for the next few days as everyone filled me in on what a disaster I am.

This time, however, there is nothing. Complete radio silence. To me, that's even more terrifying.

In the absence of any facts, I'm left only with my own conjecture as to what I did without remembering.

My stomach is growling so hard I don't even bother to

heat up the noodles, just crash-land on the couch and start shoving them into my mouth with the plastic fork.

Old, cold noodles is what I deserve, really.

The shame of it all really begins to sink in. The realization that I've broken every promise to every person I've ever loved, over and over. I think of my daughter, her sweet and shining face.

What would she think if she saw me now?

Unwashed, hunched over a box of cold noodles in the dark. Mark was right. I'm not fit to be a parent, not in this state.

I thought I was better. I really did.

My head drops down into my hands as it starts to spin again. This time, it's not from anything alcohol-related. This time, it's because I'm truly coming to understand what a mess I am.

An absolute screw-up, who has burned every bridge and wasted every second chance I've been given.

I feel empty, cavernous. Staring at the blank wall across from me in the dark, mind numbly running over my continued mistakes.

I'm not sure how long I remain like this, in this strange half-awake guilt trance, but I'm suddenly snapped out of it by a knock at the door.

My first thought is: Mark. He's finally come for an explanation of whatever horrible behavior I displayed.

Blinking to try and clear the thoughts from my mind, I push off from the couch and start toward the door. Passing by the wall-leaning standing mirror reveals my state.

It's enough to make me pause.

My hair is greasy and knotty, sticking out at all angles from my head. I'm still wearing the same ratty t-shirt I managed to pull on yesterday after stripping off my blood-stained clothes.

There's no time to change however, as Mark knocks on the door again, this time in earnest.

I must've really messed up, I think with a hard swallow. That's a cold knock, hard and unyielding.

Running a hand through my hair, I cross the rest of the room and grab hold of the door handle. I'm already forming an apology in my mind when I pull open the door.

Except as I do, I see it's not Mark standing there in the hallway. Instead, it's two police officers.

"Katherine Rose? We'd like for you to come with us, please," the officer on the left says.

"We have some questions we'd like for you to answer."

TWENTY-ONE
JUDITH

I push open the door to the police precinct building with a gloved hand.

A gust of cold air comes in with me, making me shiver as I begin to unzip my jacket in the entryway. A man behind a desk and a wall of bulletproof glass looks up at me.

"My name is Judith Rose-Wharton. Detective Scalini wanted me to come down," I say.

The officer looks down for a moment and then nods. He steps off of his chair and walks around to let me in through another door, and then I'm following him to a large back room with desks scattered around.

"Wait in the chair over there, please," the man says with a point.

It's situated at the end of a gray desk. As I come close to it, I see just how much of the paint has been rubbed off. Who knows how many people have sat here before me?

Swallowing my squeamish thoughts, I take a seat stiffly and check my phone.

Scalini said there had been an update in the case, but instead of sharing it over the phone, he said I had to come down here for some reason.

While I have the utmost respect for the police, I've never enjoyed interacting with them. I suppose there's some small fear that they might suddenly arrest me, no matter the circumstances.

Now, that might be a very real possibility. It's very important that no matter what is said, I remain ever the caring wife whose husband has mysteriously gone missing.

If they figure out that I'm hiding something, I may never step foot out of here again. I ease my hands open, conscious of the fact that someone could be watching me. I need to appear worried for my husband, not myself.

Taking a smooth inhale of breath, I calm myself. He's probably called me down here to ask some follow up questions, that's all. I'm sure it's all very routine.

My bigger issue now is what to tell Amelia. Today was the second day Daddy wasn't home, and she wanted to know why.

How can I explain any of this to a five-year-old? On our way to school, I tried to come up with an adequate explanation for her. All I ended up with was that Daddy had gone away, and I wasn't quite sure when he'd be back.

A door opens from somewhere behind me, followed by murmured conversation.

"Mrs. Wharton?"

I turn around.

Detective Scalini strides toward me, hand outstretched. We shake, and I take my seat again.

"Thanks for coming down," he says, placing a hand over his tie as he sits down at his desk.

He wheels his desk chair around so that he's closer to me. There are a couple other people at the desks around me, though none of them pays us any attention.

A phone rings, its shrill call setting me on edge.

"Have they found Mark? Is he okay?" I ask, doing my best to sound sincere.

That's what a concerned wife would ask, right? I hope I sounded genuine enough. Detective Scalini raises a hand.

"Unfortunately no, we haven't located Mark yet. However... we did come across this."

Scalini opens up a desk drawer and pulls out a plastic bag. Inside the bag is a cell phone. I recognize it instantly. It's Mark's.

That makes my heart beat a little faster. I stare at the rectangle for a moment, it's screen dark.

"The reason I wanted to have you down today was to confirm this is indeed Mark's cellphone," Scalini says.

"That is my husband's," I reply. "Where did you find it?"

I look up at the detective, and he gestures to it.

"It was found this morning in Central Park by a runner. They said they spotted it covered in leaves and off the path. Looked as if someone had tossed it aside."

"Mark?" I ask.

Scalini's face doesn't give anything away. "It was found in an area of the park called The Bramble, are you familiar with it?"

I swallow. "Yes. That is where the bench dedicated to his father is."

Scalini rubs his chin. "Right, I remember you mentioning it."

He taps the phone, and the screen lights up. The background is one of the photos taken on our fall trip just a few days ago. Mark and I in color-matched outfits, Amelia between us with a big smile as she holds a pumpkin.

That feels almost like a lifetime ago now.

"Mrs. Wharton, do you happen to know the passcode to this phone? It'd really help us in our investigation," Scalini asks me.

My thoughts race. Of course I know the passcode, but should I give it to him?

If I do, he'll have unfettered access to everything. That means texts between Mia and Mark, which might be bad for me. But that was going to come out eventually, right?

While the seconds tick by, I rack my brain, trying to think if there is anything on there that might incriminate me in some way.

Then again, if I say I don't know the code, they'll just get a warrant and open the phone anyway. I need to do everything I can to remain out of their suspicions of any wrongdoing.

So, I nod. I tell Scalini the code, and he scribbles it down into his notebook.

"So what happens now?" I ask, feeling my chest tighten.

There's an inkling of an idea in my head, but I almost don't want to hear it spoken aloud.

"Well, thanks to you, we'll be able to take a look at Mark's phone, see if anything comes up. That should give us a pretty good idea of where his head was at recently."

"In the meantime, we've already started sifting through footage taken from cameras in the area during the time window you provided us," Scalini says.

My pulse jumps, but I cover it by shifting in my chair. As inconspicuously as I can, I slide my hands beneath my jacket. They've started trembling again, thanks to the adrenaline pumping through my system.

"The cameras," I say. "I didn't realize they had any inside the park."

Scalini nods. "Oh yeah. We've added a bunch just last year to help with public safety."

Breathe. I should be breathing. *This is a good thing, Judith. Now they can track down your husband.*

I manage a thin smile. Scalini is explaining how they'll use the cameras to help narrow the timeline, but his words sound slightly distant.

Inside, my mind is racing. The cameras. Of course there are cameras in Central Park.

I have no doubt that when they look at the cameras, they are going to be able to spot Mark. This time of year, there are far fewer people walking around. The summer crowds have come and gone.

No, they'll definitely be able to find Mark on those cameras.

The problem is, there's also a good chance they're going to see me on the tape, too.

TWENTY-TWO
KATIE

There are no windows in this room.

A chill runs down my spine as I glance around the space I find myself in. I'm down at the police station, after having been escorted by the two officers who came to my door.

Neither of them told me what was going on, explaining that I would receive more information from the detective at the station.

That only served to make me more nervous. By the time I got here, I was little more than a bundle of nerves. What is going on?

The officer's stony faces revealed absolutely nothing as I sat in the back of the squad car. Total silence in the car, each second ticking by marked by higher notes of anxiety. My hands twist together as I shift in the cold chair. It's plastic and metal and heavily faded from use.

Besides the chair, there's only the table in front of me. That's it. Then four white walls and a buzzing office light overhead.

Completely barren, devoid of any answers. My eyes flick to the door to my right, which has remained shut ever since an officer escorted me inside with the promise that someone would be with me shortly.

That was almost an hour ago. I check my phone again before stuffing it back into my pocket. Three minutes short of an hour.

My mind can't help but fill with questions while I wait. Clearly, I must've done something wrong after drinking. That much is obvious.

But I've never been brought in like this before in the past. It makes me even more nervous as I wonder what happened.

More importantly, what have I *done*?

That is the question that is eating me alive. I shift again in the chair, unable to get comfortable.

It's like all my muscles want to move, run away. Try and find out exactly what's going on, and yet I can't. I'm picking at a nail, my stomach in knots when the door finally clicks open.

My attention is pulled to it in an instant.

"Ms. Rose? I'm Detective Scalini," the man says, coming forward to offer me a hand.

He's got a folder tucked under the other arm. I reach out to shake his hand, realizing too late how sweaty my palm is. The detective doesn't comment on it and takes a seat at the end of the table, so we're on a diagonal to each other.

"So. Thanks for coming down. I'm sure you'd like to hear why we called you in, Ms. Rose," Detective Scalini says.

I nod quickly. Too quickly. Should I ask for a lawyer?

"It's to do with Mark Wharton, your ex-husband," the detective says.

The world slows down. All I can hear now is my pulse in my ears as I stare at the detective.

"What... what happened? Is something wrong?" I ask, my throat dry.

"See, that's the thing we're trying to figure out, Ms. Rose," the detective replies, "Judith Wharton reported him missing yesterday."

I blink, stunned.

The words sound hollow as they reach my ears. There's so much going on right now, it feels like it hardly has any meaning behind it.

All I can think is that something happened to Mark. And then my brain finally computes the ending of the detective's sentence.

Reported missing *yesterday*.

Which means during the time I blacked out, Mark went missing.

I can hardly breathe in the cold room, my lungs seeming to shrivel up entirely. This can't be real. It doesn't feel like it is. I simply cannot be in a police interview room right now, being asked about the disappearance of my ex-husband.

And yet here I am. This is no nightmare. This is really real. It's really happening.

I blacked out. That same day, Mark didn't come home.

Something happened to him. Something that might've had to do with *me*.

My voice quivers as I somehow find the strength to speak. "Missing?"

Detective Scalini nods. "Now, I'll be honest with you here, as I was with Mrs. Wharton. In a case like Mark's, where the missing individual is an adult, with no history of mental concerns, and in the absence of any evidence suggesting foul play, it's usually given a lower priority."

I nod numbly as the detective continues.

"Not to say we do nothing, of course, but the individual, being an adult, does not legally have to come home."

I'm still staring at him, hooked on every word. Detective Scalini leans forward now, changing his position in his chair as he finds my eyes.

"Initially, it was assumed Mark had simply chosen not to come home, for whatever reason," he says.

Initially. He's saying it like things have changed. I blink, meeting the detective's gaze. I still can't speak, the lump in my throat feeling more like a mountain as I wait for Detective Scalini to continue.

"That is, until a phone was discovered by a runner this morning, pulled from the underbrush. When we turned it on, we found it belonged to Mark Wharton."

My heart is a hammer against my ribcage, making my bones hurt.

"Now, the reason we called you in today, Ms. Rose, is that when we got the phone unlocked, we discovered a few interesting things," Detective Scalini finishes.

He's sitting up all the way now and has opened up the file in front of him. Inside are a few sheets of paper. He picks up the top sheet and slides it over to me.

"This is the call log for Mark's cellphone," Detective

Scalini says. "It says here you called him almost twenty times the day he went missing."

I stare down at the sheet. Detective Scalini puts up his hands.

"Now, I just want to be absolutely clear, you're not being charged with anything, Ms. Rose. No one is. For all we know, Mark wanted a new life, and that means leaving his phone behind. We've certainly seen it before. All I'm trying to do now is make sure that's what happened."

I nod, chewing my lip. Letting out a short breath, I work to get my thoughts together.

"He... we share custody of our daughter. Amelia," I say.

"A couple days earlier, he told me he was going to try for full custody. I..."

"You were calling him to discuss the custody situation," Detective Scalini says, nodding.

My head bounces up and down. "Yes."

"I can understand that, Ms. Rose. I'm divorced myself, two children. Couple boys. Rascals, but I love them."

Somehow I manage a smile. I feel disconnected from my body right now, like this is all still some sort of bad dream. That maybe if I just go through with it, eventually my body will wake up and it'll all be over.

"So you tried to call him a bunch, but he didn't pick up. You didn't go to see him to discuss any of this?" Detective Scalini asks.

I shake my head, even as the question stings like a bee inside.

I want to scream at him that no, I have absolutely zero idea what I did or didn't do. That I was completely intoxicated and have literally no memories.

But if I do that, I get arrested instantly. Maybe even charged with murder. And right now, I still have no idea if I did anything.

There's no way I could've, right? There's no time to think about it right now, because the detective is asking me another question.

"So when was the last time you did see Mark? I'm trying to put together a general idea of his whereabouts in the days leading up to his disappearance," Detective Scalini says.

I swallow, forcing all the raging thoughts inside my head down enough so I can function. "Last Saturday. He —he came by to tell me how he and Judith were going for full custody."

Detective Scalini nods to himself as he scribbles something down. "Saturday, got it. And Judith is your... sister, right? By blood?"

"Yes," I say, rubbing my face.

He shakes his head. "I can imagine that stirring up some trouble in the family,"

He has no idea. I simply nod yes. "We don't speak now. Judith and I."

"And again, completely understandable," he says.

"Just one last question for you. I apologize, but it's protocol. Where were you the evening Mark went missing?"

The detective's question makes my stomach tighten

as I swallow. The truth? I don't remember a thing. Completely blank.

"At home. I live way out in Brooklyn," I manage.

Scalini scribbles something out and then drops his pencil.

He closes his notebook with finality. "Well, thank you for your time, Ms. Rose. We appreciate you coming down and helping us with this. We'll let you know if we need anything else from you," Scalini says, pushing out of his chair.

I stand up too, feeling shaky. It's taking everything I have to hold myself together here. Once I get back home, I can let it all out. But not here. Just not here.

He walks me back down the hallway. As we go, my eyes travel to the left, where a door sits open. My chest tightens as I see who is sitting inside.

My eyes connect with my sister's, our gazes meeting for the first time in years.

TWENTY-THREE
JUDITH

I blink, my entire body stiff.

That was Katie in the hallway. It's been almost two years since I've seen her, but I know that was her.

She looked awful, worse than I think I've ever seen her.

"Thanks Mrs. Wharton, we're all set. We really appreciate your cooperation," the officer seated across from me says.

They had me recount the timeline once again, even though I feel like I've been over things a dozen times by this point. Now I'm wondering if Scalini kept me here on purpose.

Maybe for that moment just now, between my sister and me. It can't simply be coincidence they just happened to walk by this room with the door open when they did, right?

Does that mean Scalini suspects something? Suspects Katie?

Suspects *me*?

That is enough to make my skin prickle.

My hands run down the length of my thighs, and then I stand up. Now that I've started thinking about it, it seems more and more clear that Scalini might suspect me of something.

The officer across the table from me reveals nothing, the two of us exiting the interview room and coming back into the main room.

I look around for my sister, but it looks like she's already left. That at least allows me a moment to breathe. Both of us being brought in makes me wonder.

Is it just because Scalini wants a better picture of Mark's life, as he's been insisting, or does he suspect foul play?

I wish I had the answer. Maybe I'd be able to relax if I did.

I'm rigid as I move through the police station, eyes focused on the door in front of me. They called me in here to get the password to Mark's phone, but what if that wasn't all?

Pulling out my phone, I check the time. I'm going to be very late for work today. If I—

I run into the back of someone who's suddenly stopped abruptly in front of me, my phone clattering down to the floor in the lobby.

Great. Just great. The person turns around as I reach down to pick up my phone, their large raincoat swishing.

Our eyes meet, and I freeze with my fingertips touching the phone. It's Katie.

There are heavy bags under my sister's eyes and lines across her face that I don't remember. It's only been two years, but she looks like she's aged a decade during that time.

Stiffening, I scoop up my phone as Katie zips up her jacket the rest of the way and heads outside, leaving me alone in the lobby.

The door opening brings in a sheet of rain that coats the floor mat in front of me and makes the tile glisten with water. I watch the back of her as she steps outside.

That was the closest we'd been in over two years. Standing right across from each other. Then she's gone, her raincoat disappearing into the sea of other coats and umbrellas on the sidewalk outside.

I fumble around in my purse for my umbrella. The longer I stay here, the more guilty I feel. If Scalini does suspect someone did something to Mark, I need to be prepared. I make a mental note to research lawyers today. Just in case.

I will not be going down for this. Letting out a breath, I get my umbrella open.

I've got to relax. Most of this is probably conjecture in my head. As usual, I'm here crafting battleplans for a war that has not even begun yet.

And may never begin. Scalini *asked* me to come down, he didn't make me.

Besides, all they've found is a phone. That doesn't really prove anything one way or another. There is no reason to think that they might suspect me of anything.

After all, I've been very helpful, haven't I?

I'm sure there are going to be more questions when they look through Mark's phone and find the texts between him and the schoolteacher. I've got to work on my surprised face.

It's got to be believable when they ask me if I knew anything about the affair. Anything less, and Scalini might think I had something to do with this.

Add that to the list.

It's going to be a busy next few days, that's for sure. Lots to do.

My mind scurries as I head down the sidewalk, wind blowing rain up against my umbrella.

I'm back in control now though. Now that I'm outside the station, it feels like I have time to plan.

Planning is what I do best, after all.

Right now, no one is saying I've done anything. They see me as the concerned wife of a missing husband.

If I play this just right, that'll stay the case.

I'm barely able to get outside the police station and stagger down into the subway before breaking into tears.

It's just too overwhelming. Mark is missing, vanished —and I might've had something to do with it.

No, that's not harsh enough. It's not just that I might've had something to do with it—I might've been the one who did it.

My chest aches. The world spins around me as I collapse onto a wooden bench in the subway.

It feels like it's a million degrees down here, a combination of the trapped heat, the mass of bodies, and the overwhelming sense of panic that is flooding my entire system.

I blacked out the exact day my ex-husband went missing. Waking up the next morning, there was dirt under my nails.

Why was there dirt under my nails?

Even thinking about it makes me sick. I sit up a little in the hard wooden bench seat, catching the eye of the woman sitting beside me. There's a look of judgement there, just like I saw in Judith's eyes. She's probably wondering what substance this jittery mess of a human being is on.

Looking away, I chew my lip. My leg is pumping up and down as my thoughts race, and I can't stop it.

I can't stop anything. It's like the floodgates have been opened in my mind, allowing a reservoir of fear to flow freely.

I was so angry at Mark. So angry. Angrier than I think I've ever been.

I wanted him to pay for what he was trying to do to me. My stomach turns over.

Did I get drunk enough that I actually went through with it? The timing is just too specific to be coincidental.

Running my palms down my soaked jeans, I bite so hard on my lip that I draw blood. A hiss escapes my throat as the coppery taste of blood fills my mouth.

What do I do?

Part of me wants to march back into the police station and tell the detective the truth. That really I have no clue where I was or what I was doing at the time of Mark's disappearance. Only that I woke up the next day with a serious hangover, covered in blood and dirt. That I've been spending my time standing outside his apartment building, watching him.

That'd be enough to lock me up, wouldn't it?

Maybe it'd be for the best. If I did do something to Mark, it's clear that I shouldn't be around people. It's not safe for them.

I can't control my drinking, and it looks like I might not be able to control what happens when I drink either.

But what if I *didn't* do it?

I want to cling onto that hope desperately, even though there isn't any solid proof to the contrary. I couldn't have done something to Mark, right? Not really.

Yes, I've done plenty of bad things when I've been intoxicated in the past. I've definitely hurt people, but never physically. Not like this.

I'm not a violent person, am I?

A subway train rumbles into the station, the hot, sticky tube filling with noise as it blasts past and begins to slow amid the sound of squealing brakes. People move en masse toward the subway car doors.

They open, and bodies flow in and out. I remain rooted to my seat on the bench, unable to move.

My legs feel incapable of taking another step, not right now. I'm battling myself in my own mind, trying to figure out what I've done—or didn't do.

Tears sting at my eyes and I wipe at them, cheeks burning with embarrassment even though I don't think anyone even remotely cares.

They're too busy with their own lives, their own concerns. Something tells me I've got bigger concerns than their opinions right now.

Wiping my eyes again, I try to sit up a little higher. If only I could remember what happened during my blackout. If only I knew definitively what I did.

It's the not knowing that is the real torture. The black hole of possibility that leaves endless space for my anxious mind to fill in the gaps.

And just about everything my mind can come up with is terrifying.

Everyone around me moves with purpose, umbrellas dripping and raincoats slick as they jostle for position.

I wish I had somewhere to go. All that waits for me at home is an empty apartment and more of these overpowering thoughts.

Thoughts like I very well might have *murdered* my ex-husband.

TWENTY-FIVE

JUDITH

The pounding at the door alarms me.

I didn't get a call from the front desk. Why wouldn't they have called?

"Hello?" I ask, my throat tightening.

"Judith Rose-Wharton, this is the New York Police Department. Please open the door," a man shouts harshly.

My heart pounds against my ribcage as I remain frozen on the couch. The police are here. Why are the police here?

Yesterday at the station, everything was cordial. What's changed? What did they find?

"Open this door, or we will break it down," the man shouts again.

There are more shouts in the hallway. I'm supposed to go and open up the door, but I can't. All I can think is that I haven't had enough time.

There wasn't enough time to plan out everything I

was going to say. I remain on the couch, even as the thudding grows louder.

They're here right now. For me. By the sounds of it, they're breaking down the door.

It flies inward, making me jump. Uniformed officers flood into the apartment, fanning out as Detective Scalini makes his way toward me.

There's something in his hand. Sheets of paper. He extends them out toward me as he speaks.

"Mrs. Wharton, this is a warrant to search the property," he says.

I accept the stack of paper, leafing through it. I have no idea what I'm looking at as Scalini barks orders over my head.

"You two—bedroom. Riviera, check the bathroom. I need someone to look through laundry too."

"What's going on?" I ask, finally getting over my shock enough to manage speech.

It's rare that I'm caught off-guard like this. I expected the detective to call me in for another meeting to discuss the findings on Mark's phone, not to have the police bust down my front door.

I'm quickly recovering, though—and already thinking of which lawyer I'll call.

Scalini looks down at me. "We spent yesterday combing through Mark's phone for anything that might help explain his disappearance."

He steps forward, pulling a folded sheet of paper out of his suit jacket pocket.

"Is there anything you'd like to tell me, Mrs. Wharton?"

I unfold the sheet of paper slowly, my throat dry. It's a print-out of an email draft.

My name is Mark Wharton. If you're reading this, then that means I'm already dead.

Someone is out there. I can hear them. I think they're coming for me.

I know I haven't lived a perfect life. I don't think any of us have. I've made my fair share of mistakes.

*But right now, I can only think of two people who would kill me over those mistakes. If I'm dead, then it was by the hand of one of the **Rose sisters**.*

I'm hiding right now, but if

I stiffen as my eyes reach the end of the draft. Any sense of calm I'd managed to recover after the shock of the police department's sudden intrusion has swiftly vanished.

Scalini sits down on the couch beside me as my heart thuds.

"We found this in Mark's drafts. Looks like he was typing it out shortly before something happened to him—possibly moments before, given the incomplete sentence at the end," Scalini says.

He looks at me with hard eyes. Behind him, police officers are busy tearing apart my life.

"There is another team at your sister's apartment right now, doing the same thing. If there's anything you want to tell me, now is your last chance," Scalini says.

"I... I would like an attorney present," I say.

"Fair enough. I think you'll need one, with this note," Scalini says.

I can't stop watching the officers rushing around my

apartment. They move with such swiftness and precision. If there was anything incriminating hidden here, I have no doubt they would find it. I watch two of them go through the drawers in the kitchen, rifling through our silverware. The sharp clanging is replaced with a dull thump as the drawer is slammed shut.

"I have to say Mrs. Wharton, this is a first for me," Scalini says, "sisters sharing one husband. Now the husband's gone missing. Sounds like something straight out of a thriller novel."

I don't respond, keeping my hands clasped in front of me as I breathe evenly. It's not like I love having these people rifling through my home, but at least I know they won't find anything.

All I have to do is endure this discomfort, meet with my lawyer, and he will instruct me on how to proceed.

Repeating this to myself, I'm able to slow my heartrate back down to a reasonable level as well, as much as Scalini seems intent on disrupting it.

"Detective Scalini," an officer says from the other side of the room.

Both of us turn to him. He's standing by the television, directing a flashlight into the narrow space behind it. I know what he's discovered.

"Looks like there's a safe back here," the officer says.

Scalini turns to me. "We'll need that code, Mrs. Wharton."

There's a glimmer in his eye, like he thinks he's caught me. I glance over at him.

Do I have to open it for him? He seems to sense my

unspoken question and taps on the warrant on the coffee table.

"Access to everything, Mrs. Wharton. Wouldn't do us much good if the bad guys could just hide the murder weapon in the safe, would it?"

He's right. They have a warrant, which means I have to comply or face charges.

Scalini pushes off the couch and heads across the room, rounding the coffee table and chairs before coming to a stop beside the TV.

Directing another officer to join the first, he watches as the two of them grab hold of the television. The men ease it upward, the wall mount carrying the load until it's a good two feet higher, revealing the safe built into the wall.

"Code, please," Scalini says to me.

I give it to him, my chest still tight. I'm seated again, hands clasped in front of me. Scalini gets the safe open, his back to me as he rifles around inside.

A moment later, he turns around.

Our eyes meet, and for a second I almost want to smile. He looks disappointed, so certain he would find something inside.

"Either way, we're going to be digging deep into your life, Mrs. Wharton. You and your sister both," Scalini says.

"I'm going to map out every second of your life over the past few days. Wherever you went, whatever you did, I'm going to find out," he vows with his arms crossed.

My throat closes up again, though I'm careful to keep my face even. He seems to be studying me, watching me closely after everything he says. Like he wants to gauge my reaction.

I'm coming to understand that Scalini is not a man to be underestimated. It appears as though he has more on the ball than I gave him credit for initially, and that's my fault.

I should've been more prepared. They caught me off balance today.

But I've recovered now.

Scalini is not going to win. I simply will not let it happen.

Then an officer calls out, her tone excited.

"Detective Scalini," the woman says, "I've found something."

TWENTY-SIX

KATIE

I stare in shock at the TV.

There is the picture of my sister, staring back at me with those harsh eyes of hers. It's a professional photograph, judging by the background. Below the photo is the headline WOMAN ARRESTED IN DISAPPEARANCE OF HUSBAND.

It doesn't feel real. All of this is like some strange dream, only I can't wake up. Tears of relief and terror roll down my face at once.

The news anchor continues sharing details of the case, explaining how Mark's wedding ring was discovered in Judith's purse after a search of their apartment.

On the ring were traces of Mark's blood. I run a hand through my hair as I sit back, stunned.

A family photo replaces the image of Judith. It's her and Mark and Amelia, all of them dressed up and smiling as they stand among piles of pumpkins. Amelia is in the center, holding a pumpkin high as she grins widely.

That makes my throat tighten even more. My baby

girl, caught in the middle of this. She's with Mark's mother right now, and I can't imagine what she's feeling.

I want to go to her, but I can't. Not like this.

It's like I'm experiencing every possible emotion all at once. I don't know whether to feel immense relief, or complete horror, or just utter shock.

Judith killed Mark, not me.

But Judith *killed* Mark. *Killed* him.

I literally saw her a couple days ago at the station, looked her in the eyes. She had slaughtered the man I loved, and there she was, proper and put-together as ever.

She doesn't even seem human in my mind right now. I mean, she's always been cold and calculating, but this...

We grew up together. That is my *sister* I'm looking at on the television screen right now, who's just been arrested for the murder of her husband.

My husband.

All of this is just too insane.

As crazy and as devastating as it is, there's this guilty feeling of near-delirium at the fact that it wasn't me who did it.

When the police were here yesterday searching the apartment, I could hardly breathe. Because I didn't even know the truth myself. I kept thinking what if they did find something, something that proved I was the one who had hurt Mark?

But apparently their search revealed nothing. If it had, I'd be in a jail cell right now, waiting to be assigned a court-appointed lawyer.

Instead, I was left to just sit in my apartment and

keep wondering, keep twisting myself into mental knots trying to unlock the hidden memories.

Until today.

My sister. My baby sister has killed someone.

The perfect Rose no longer.

Reaching forward with a shaking hand, I grab my cup of tap water and sip it. I almost feel like I need to pick up the phone and tell someone about all of this, but then I realize there's no one to tell.

Mom and Dad are gone, and it's not like I'm very close with any of my cousins anymore. I have no friends left. I've alienated just about everyone I've ever known.

The only one who even seemed to tolerate me was Mark, and that was probably only because of Amelia.

Now he's gone, too.

A new thought takes hold in my brain. A sick thought. I'm disgusted at myself immediately for even thinking it.

But it's there, feeling a bit like hope and bit like I'm morbidly dancing on Mark's grave.

There's no way the court case to take Amelia from me will go through now. Will it?

I shake myself. Mark is dead, and here I am almost celebrating. My eyes shut as I lean back against the couch.

I'm trying to picture him in my mind, but all I can come up with is the memory of him staring at me with that look of deep sadness on his face.

You're out of chances, Katie.

I've lost track at this point of how many chances he

gave me. How many times I screwed up, and yet there he was, willing to listen and forgive and let me try again.

Even after we divorced.

If the past couple days have taught me anything, it's that Mark was right. I shouldn't be around Amelia. I blacked out and lost nearly twenty-four hours, for goodness sakes.

And yet I hated him for saying it. For telling me the truth.

Hated him enough that I wanted him dead. My stomach turns.

I got my wish, and now I hate it. I absolutely hate it.

I think I might hate myself even more. I collapse to the side of the couch, only half-watching the TV as I sob against the cushions.

This can't be real, can it?

I desperately just want to wake up. Open my eyes and find Mark sleeping soundly beside me. Amelia is in the other room, already awake and playing with her toys.

We'll have breakfast as a family, and then I'll give Mark a big kiss as he heads off to work.

They're showing another photo of Mark on the TV. He's grinning at Amelia, those adorable dimples of his shining through. He'll never get to smile at her again.

I think of her right now, how scared and sad and confused she must be.

My baby girl. I failed her so completely. If I hadn't had such an issue with drinking, none of this would've happened.

We never would've gotten divorced, he never would've married Judith. She never would've killed him.

All of this is my fault.

Mine.

TWENTY-SEVEN

KATIE

I blink, jerking a little as I pull myself out of a stupor.

I'm holding an orange. Why am I holding an orange?

Looking up, I find that I'm at the grocery store. When did I get here? I've got a cart beside me, but there's nothing in it.

The past few days have been nothing but a long, dreary blur. The rain has not let up, and neither has the news coverage.

Judith was discovered on the Central Park security tapes. They've matched her hat and coat to the ones in the video. There's no footage of her leaving, which means she must've exited the park a different way.

It seems like the whole city is talking about it. The perfect family, shattered.

The news articles love to point out how perfect everything appeared in their relationship. *Trouble in paradise*, one article wrote.

Shouldn't believe everything you see on social media, another lamented.

In a third article, some psychiatrist named Dr. DeLuca breaks down Judith's psychological profile.

It's like a frenzy. Everyone is obsessed with the perfect New York family that wasn't. Those beautiful fall family photos of the three of them seem to be everywhere online and on my TV every time I turn it on.

I've had at least a dozen news reporters and online blogs reach out to me for comment. Obviously, I turned them all down.

Watching reality TV is entertaining. Watching *your* reality become TV isn't. At all.

This was Mark's life, and perfect strangers are coming up with theories and writing about his life and death like they knew him. Like they knew any of us.

I've read the stories about our supposed "love triangle" too. I always thought the news was supposed to be solely about the facts, not this speculation rumor mill.

All of it is just so surreal.

Even though I know it's not the case, it feels like everyone in the world is talking about it. I even had a couple former coworkers who swore they'd never speak to me again texting me, asking about everything.

I set down the orange and take a breath. Sleep has been near impossible the past few days. Not with everything on my mind.

Though I know it's not good for me, I can't stop reading articles and watching the news. It's a horrible feeling, being so close and yet so far away from what's happening.

Everyone involved in the case, I know intimately, and yet I'm just as clueless as the rest of the city as to what comes next. I can only sit and watch with my stomach tight and my heart heavy.

Making my way to the frozen foods section of the grocery store, I grab as many microwaveable meals as I can afford.

It's all I can do to put one of these in the microwave to feed myself these days. That's if I remember to eat at all.

Back at home, the first thing I do is turn the TV back on. I've had it on quite literally nonstop since this whole thing began. They aren't talking about Mark right now, though. There's some flooding happening in The Bronx due to the rain.

Honestly, it's a good reminder. This isn't actually the center of everyone else's life, like it is mine.

Most people have probably seen the story by now, or maybe read something on their phone about a wife murdering her husband. Maybe they read one article and then promptly forgot about it and went on with their day.

I wish I could do that. I know it's what I should do, for more reasons than one.

Living like this is not healthy, not sustainable. I'm running out of money, my body is completely exhausted, and I can hardly think straight.

But I need to know more.

I need to know why. How.

Landing on the couch, I pull out my phone and search the case on my phone's internet browser.

I've clicked on all the links that come up but do so again. A couple have updates, but it's mostly corrections and minor spelling error fixes. Nothing substantial.

I don't know what I'm wanting to see, really. It feels almost like a gruesome car crash, in that I know I should look away, but I can't.

In a way it's my family that's in the car, making it all the more impossible to pull myself away.

My stomach rumbles, so I go to the fridge and get out one of the microwaveable meals. As I toss it into the microwave, I hear my phone buzz against the couch. Racing back over to it, I scoop it up.

A text from Mark's mother, Doris. We haven't interacted with each other since the divorce.

She says Amelia would like to see me.

I swallow hard, my hands shaking a little as I read over the text. Tomorrow is Saturday, after all. The weekend, when I should have visitation.

Given everything going on with me though, I don't know how good an idea it is to see my daughter, as desperately as I want to.

The condition I'm in is not something I want her to see, not how I want her to think of her mother. I chew on my lip in indecision as the microwave hums along behind me.

What am I saying? My daughter wants to see me. I'm not going to turn that down, no matter what.

I blow out a breath and glance into the glass door of the microwave at my reflection. It isn't pretty.

My hair sticks out at all angles, and I'm fairly sure the stain on this t-shirt is left over from some TV dinner pasta I had three nights back.

If I'm going to see Amelia, I need to pull myself together.

If I won't do it for myself, I'll do it for my daughter. I can't let her see me like this. Not when everything else in her life is falling apart.

Now is my chance to be there for her. A chance to make up for all the times in the past I couldn't be. She literally doesn't have anyone else.

That thought is enough to put a spark of energy into my body. Amelia needs me.

Leaving the meal in the microwave, I walk right to the bathroom and get the shower turned on. It takes a couple minutes, but soon hot water is shooting out of the shower head, and steam fills up the small bathroom.

I shut my eyes and breathe it in, allowing the damp heat to envelop me. Amelia needs her mother now more than ever, and I'm going to be there for her.

No matter what, I'm going to be there.

After a long, long shower, I feel human again. I wasn't just washing off sweat and dirt, I was cleansing myself of all the dark thoughts that have become encrusted in my mind during the past few days.

It's time for them to go. I cannot allow myself to spiral out now, for Amelia's sake. She needs me.

That simple knowledge is enough. I put on a fresh pair of jeans and a shirt and feel better than I have in weeks as I eat dinner.

Mark's mom lives way out in Queens, in the same house that he grew up in. I haven't been there in quite a few years, but I still remember how to get there.

Doris hasn't texted me since the initial message, so I respond, saying I'll be there and giving her an ETA.

It feels good. Somehow, hearing that my daughter needs me has brought me back from the brink.

I won't fail her. Not now.

THE SUBWAY SYSTEM in Queens isn't nearly as extensive as it is in Manhattan, so once I get off at the stop, I've got to walk almost twenty minutes before I reach the house.

It's much more suburban here, given how much more space there is in Queens. Brick townhomes with driveways line both sides of the street as I walk. A car drives by me, pushing rainwater up onto the sidewalk in a watery wall that has me side-stepping to avoid being soaked.

At least it stopped raining today. The sky is still a bleak gray overhead, but rain isn't falling. I trudge forward, my rainboots squeaking a little on the sidewalk.

Once the car passes, the world around me falls into a quiet that doesn't feel quite right for New York City. In fact, as I look around, I realize I'm the only person in sight.

Even though it's not raining, there's definitely still a damp chill in the air. I zip up my jacket a little more and force my hands deeper into the pockets of my jeans. Almost there.

As I turn onto the street, there's a brief moment of panic in my tired brain as I realize I might've forgotten which house was actually hers.

But then I see it, and my shoulders lower. The front of it has a brick base like many of the others, but the second floor has yellowed clapboard siding that I recognize. It's faded a lot since I first laid eyes on the place.

That same oil stain is still on the driveway, too. I walk up to the rusted front gate and pull it open. The hinge lets out a squeak, grating against my ears as I slip through the opening.

There's no sound but my footsteps as I walk up to the staircase that leads to the front door. To my right is the garage, its door closed.

My heart is beating faster now. I climb the steps and come up to the front door, which has a wrought-iron door guard in front. My finger presses the doorbell button, and then I wait.

My throat is dry as I listen to the familiar chime echo through the house.

A moment later, I hear Amelia shout for Doris, letting her know someone is at the door. Her voice brings an instant smile to my face, and my eyes fill with tears. It's a mix of excitement and worry and everything else all balled into one.

There's shuffling, and then the door behind the guard comes open. Doris stands in the entryway, wearing black.

"Mommy," Amelia says from the hallway behind her.

"Hey sweetheart," I say, my voice catching in my throat.

Doris and I were never close, even before Mark and I divorced. She definitely wasn't a monster-in-law, but I'd honestly always wished she liked me a little bit more.

Mark said he didn't care what she thought of me, but to me, it mattered.

Doris gives me a nod and unlocks the door guard so I

can step inside. I let out a shiver as Amelia bounds up to me, throwing her arms around my legs in a tight hug.

"Hi Mommy, I missed you," she says, burrowing into me.

That makes the tears sting even more. I squeeze her back with just as much intensity and relief.

"I missed you too, baby. So, so much."

"Come see what Gammie and I have been making," she says, taking off for the kitchen.

"I'll be in in just a second," I call after her as I undo the zipper of my jacket.

"Hello Doris," I say with a nod, "Thank you for the text. It really means a—"

"I didn't do it for you," Doris says quietly, interrupting me as she takes my coat.

"I didn't want to ever see you again, but Amelia needs support right now," she adds.

My former mother-in-law finishes hanging my coat in the tiny coat closet and turns back to me. As she speaks again, I see that she is fighting back tears.

"My baby boy is gone. *Gone*. I don't care what the news says—I blame both of you."

Then she's walking back toward the kitchen, leaving me standing in the entryway blinking hard with my mouth hanging open. I feel like I've been stung, her words cutting right into me.

Doris says something to Amelia as she enters the kitchen, but I'm still trying to recover and can't fully make out the words.

My chest starts to constrict, and I almost feel like I'm

going to start hyperventilating. But then I hear Amelia giggle and manage to get control of myself.

For her, I need to remain calm. Doris is just hurting right now, like all of us are. Her only son was murdered, after all. I... I shouldn't take it personally.

Running a hand under my nose, I take one last breath and then trail after her into the kitchen at the back of the house.

"Look—look—what we made," Amelia says as soon as she sees me, oblivious to the tense exchange between her grandmother and me.

She's gesturing toward a plate of maple leaf-shaped cookies, each covered in colored sugar so that they're all yellow and brown and orange and red. I manage a smile. "Wow, those look delicious. Did you decorate them yourself?"

Amelia nods proudly. I glance over at Doris, who seems to be working hard not to look at me. Her words echo again in my mind.

I blame both of you.

I do my best to shake off the cruel remark, trying to engage with Amelia as I help her get the cookies into the hot oven to bake.

Though she basically ignores me, Doris is exceptionally sweet to Amelia, as always. It's good to know my daughter has been well cared for and is safe and happy here.

After the cookies are in, Amelia wants to watch her favorite princess movie on the TV in the basement room. We've seen it easily three hundred times by now, but that doesn't stop her from enjoying it every time.

I had shows like that myself when I was little, comfort-watches that never got old. If there was ever a time for a comfort-watch, it's now.

We settle onto the couch downstairs, which is piled high with blankets and pillows. Amelia seems okay, at least from what I can tell.

As we get the movie started, I poke her in the ribs. She lets out a giggle.

"How are you?" I ask her.

"Good," she says.

I chew my lip. "Did... did Gammie tell you about Daddy? And Judith?"

Amelia nods, reaching for a pillow while her eyes remain glued to the television. "Daddy and Judith got into a big fight. I'm 'sposed to stay here with Gammie until they become okay again."

That forces more tears to my eyes as I nod silently. She's so innocent, and she deserves absolutely none of this. I run my hand through her silky, fine hair as we watch the movie.

"Mommy," Amelia says with a giggle, shaking me off.

"Sorry baby. I just love you so much," I say in a voice barely above a whisper.

Then I clear my throat. I need to pull myself together here. Wiping at my eyes, I slap my arms.

"Why don't I check on the cookies, and bring them down if they're ready? What do you say?" I ask her.

"Yeah," Amelia says excitedly.

I walk back up the stairs, still swiping my hand across my eyes and working to get myself back under control.

I'm here with Amelia right now, and I need to be the most present Mommy I can be.

Doris is sitting at the kitchen table as I come up from the basement. In front of her is a framed photo of Mark's high school picture. She stiffens noticeably as I enter the kitchen.

"Checking on the cookies," I say, just to fill the air between us.

Doris nods once, her eyes looking away from me. I bite my lip and then sit down across from her at the table. She looks up in surprise.

"I just wanted to say how sorry I am, about all of this. I can't even imagine what you must be going through, Doris. I just... what you said earlier... you're right. It is my fault too. If I had just been normal, we would still be married, and none of this would've ever happened," I say, my voice breaking as tears start to flow down my cheeks.

A tear slips from Doris's eye as well. She looks down at Mark's picture again.

"He was all I had," she says.

I reach across the table and take hold of her hand. Surprisingly, she doesn't yank it away.

"You still have Amelia. And I see so much of him in her," I say, finding her eyes.

Doris nods, a watery smile breaking through the despair on her face as her eyes glisten.

"I do too. I really do."

We stay like that for another couple seconds, our hands touching. It's the most we've connected with each other, ever.

Finally Doris pulls away, sniffling loudly as she pulls a tissue from her pocket.

"Thank you for coming, Katie. I know it means the world to Amelia."

"Of course. Thank you for allowing me to come."

"It's just... it's been so hard with her, you know? Trying to figure out how to explain all of this to a five year old."

"And school is another issue," she adds. "Who knows what the other kids might say to her?"

"I know." I nod in sympathy. I've thought of that myself. Hopefully the other parents have enough sense to keep their small children away from the news.

"Her teacher was nice enough to come by earlier and drop off some work for her," Doris says. "Sweet girl. Too bad she's planning to move away soon. Amelia really likes her."

I nod again. It really is too bad. The last thing my daughter needs at this point is more upheaval.

Doris lets out a heavy breath. "I just don't understand it. That's what I keep coming back to. Why would anyone want to kill my Mark?"

TWENTY-EIGHT
KATIE

I can't stop asking why myself.

That's the question that eats away at me continually, and Doris' remark spurs my own confusion to new life.

Why did Judith kill Mark?

She's always been very unforgiving, but what could he have possibly done that would warrant this?

Judith was always the more rational of the two of us. While I seemed to fly off the handle at times, it was always Judith who was able to remove emotion from any situation.

And yet she's the Rose sister who killed Mark, not me.

Being at home alone amid all this is torture. There's nowhere to go, and no one to see. Sitting inside in the dark, surrounded only by my own thoughts and the warbling of the TV is a nightmare.

I've got to try and see Judith. I just need to ask. I just need to know why.

The chances she'll actually talk to me are kind of

slim, seeing as we haven't spoken in over two years. There's a lot of bad blood between us.

But she is my sister, and maybe there's a chance she'll tell me the truth.

My hands twist together as I ride the subway up to the precinct where Judith is being held. The subway car squeals as it whistles down the tracks.

No one speaks around me, their heads buried in their phones or with headphones in. I'm too nervous to do anything but stare at the floor, my mind going over every possible way this could play out.

I might show up and she refuses to see me. That's entirely possible. In fact, I might just be the last person in the world she wants to see.

But I need to hear it from her. I need to see for myself how my own sister could be such a monster.

Will she apologize to me?

I've never known Judith to be an apologetic person, but then again, I've also never known her to fail at anything.

The hard plastic chair in the visitation room has no give to it as I lower myself into it. There's a dull buzz from somewhere I can't see, and then a flash of orange catches my attention. Judith is escorted forward, accompanied by a uniformed guard.

I have to stop my mouth from dropping open when I see her. I don't think I've seen her not looking entirely perfect and put-together since junior high.

Without makeup and sporting the bright orange prison jumpsuit, Judith looks almost like a different person altogether.

Gone is the woman who always wins. Who has the answers.

Judith sits down across from me, and then her head comes up.

Our eyes meet through the scratched translucent divider, holding each other's gazes for a moment. I don't know what I'm supposed to be feeling.

My throat tightens a little as we look each other over.

It's been a long, long time.

Shakily, I reach for the phone so we can communicate. Judith picks up the receiver on her side as well in a stiff movement.

My mouth opens, but nothing comes out. There's a little bit of static through the line as I wait for Judith to speak.

"Have you come here to gloat?" she says.

I stare back at her, feeling my heart beat quicken a little. The hostility in her tone scorches any of the pity I might've felt for her coming in.

To think I actually felt bad for her, despite what she's done, what she's taken from me.

I shift in my chair, my grip tightening on the phone. "Maybe I should."

Judith shakes her head. "Congratulations. You're no longer the biggest disappointment in the family."

Her eyes narrow. "Though I suppose it's what you wanted, isn't it? Seeing me fail. You've always hated me for being better than you."

My pulse rushes to my ears as I stare at my sister. Even wearing prison orange and looking almost like a stranger, she still has that trademark hate-ability.

I let out a scoff. "You really are unbelievable, you know that? I can't believe I ever tolerated you."

Judith's lips curl into a snarl. "Oh, I gave up tolerating you a long, long time ago."

"Was that before or after you ruined my marriage?" I hiss.

My face is hot. I know I shouldn't let her get to me like this, but I can't help myself.

"After you keep trying to ruin *mine*," Judith fires back.

"Looks to me like you already handled that yourself," I reply.

Her nostrils flare. "So they say."

My eyes bore into her.

"You're really going to try and tell me you didn't do it? They found the ring in *your* purse, Judith. Not to mention the video of you following Mark into the park that day," I say.

Judith exhales a harsh shot of breath, her lips curling.

"Of course you wouldn't believe me. In fact, maybe you had something to do with this. I wouldn't put it past you with your drinking."

I squeeze the telephone. "I wish you weren't my sister."

"Believe me, the feeling is entirely mutual," Judith hisses back.

I nod once. "Okay. Have a nice life."

My head is shaking as I slam the phone back down onto the receiver.

I've heard enough. It's clear Judith has no interest in apologizing for what she's done.

Coming here was a mistake. It was foolish of me to think that just because she'd finally lost, she might have changed and become a different person.

If anything, it feels like she's doubled down on the nastiness. Some sort of absolute refusal to accept defeat, even when the war is long past over.

Only there is no war. This is a game she's playing entirely by herself in whatever crazy, messed-up world she lives in. I push the chair back and stand, chest rising and falling as our eyes meet again.

"Bye forever, Sis," I say, giving her a mock wave.

Then I spin on my heel and walk away. I shouldn't have come.

I'm realizing now we're sisters in name only. I have absolutely nothing in common with that person behind the glass. Clearly, we can't stand each other.

Moreover, I don't *want* to stand her. I'm done.

This was the last straw. Judith can rot in here now for all I care. Any bond we might've once shared is well and truly dead.

I spend the subway ride home chewing my lip as I run through our conversation in my mind. Even now, I can still feel my hands clenching as I think about how she spoke to me.

She's the one in jail for murder, and still she tried to insult me. That's what I get for trying to extend an olive branch.

Well, I've learned my lesson.

My stop arrives quickly, thanks to being lost in my thoughts. A blustering wind blows through me as I step out of the subway, making my teeth chatter. I zip up my jacket a little more and try to put Judith out of mind.

I won't let her ruin the rest of my life. The only way I think I'll be able to get through all of this is to put my mind on something else. But what?

My apartment is dark as I unlock the door and step inside. Letting out a sigh, I throw myself down on the couch and pull out my phone. I stare blankly at the screen, just wanting to turn my brain off for a few hours.

For whatever reason, my mind keeps wanting to shift back to Judith, but I'm done, and so is she. We're no longer sisters, and I just need to forget about her.

Turning on the TV, I and put on my favorite show, but I'm only half-watching the episodes. Eventually my eyelids get heavy, so I get myself ready for sleep and climb into bed.

I don't drift right off, though. Instead, it seems like by removing the TV and phone, I've only opened up the bandwidth in my brain to think about everything again.

Even as I try to push the conversation with my sister out of mind, there's one part that sticks with me. Somewhere amid all the declarations of hatred, the snide remarks, Judith claimed she didn't do it.

Or at least, tried to, but I wouldn't hear her out. I swallow and flip so that I'm staring up at the ceiling again.

What if she was actually telling the truth?

I sit up in bed as my heart pounds. My mind fills in the darkness around me with the dirt I found under my nails the morning after Mark went missing.

I still don't know what I did.

Guilt wracks me, a feeling so overwhelming I can't stay still. My own mind is fighting against me, blaming me, hating me.

I just want it to stop. Judith did it. That's what the charge against her says.

But *she* said she didn't.

What if I did, and now I've ruined *both* Mark and Judith's lives? What if I am the monster?

My hands come up to my head as I put my feet onto the floor. There are just so many thoughts. If I don't do something, I'm not going to sleep at all.

My eyes drift over to the cabinet across the room. Almost as if pulled by a magnet, I'm back on my feet, and then I'm walking over to it.

The thoughts are just so loud. So awful. The worst part is, I don't know what's true and what's not. What if Judith wasn't lying?

Next thing I know, the cabinet door is open. Even though it's dark, I know exactly what's in there. The half-empty bottle of vodka from the last time I drank.

I know I should have emptied it into the sink. And I wanted to.

My eyes slowly adjust to the darkness as the bottle comes into view. Just a sip, that's all.

There's an ache throughout my entire body as I lay eyes on the bottle, a yearning unlike anything I've ever felt. Just one little—

I slam the cabinet door shut. I can't. I should just go back to bed and throw the covers over my head and hope I eventually pass out.

Pulling open the fridge, my apartment is cast in the

yellowed glow from the small light bulb inside. There's nothing to eat in here. I close the fridge and take a heavy breath. It's not food that I want anyway.

If I stay in this apartment with that bottle, I don't think I'll be able to resist much longer. Throwing on a coat, I wrench open my front door and stumble out into the hallway.

It's late, but this is NYC after all. I'll find some late-night diner and just eat something sugary and terrible for me. That's supposed to help stem the craving for alcohol, right?

Outside of my building, the night air is brutally cold. I suck in a breath as I step out. It's got to be like forty degrees out right now.

I start marching toward a diner I know of nearby. Maybe a burger, a shake, and...

My feet have frozen in place as I look across the street at the sign above the door of a bar. Its neon bulbs glow brightly in the pitch black around me. Suddenly my lips are dry.

I know I shouldn't have any hard liquor, and I'm set on that. But maybe I can have just one beer. I can handle that.

Just something to satiate the craving, and then I'll move on. A way to dull the incessant circular thoughts enough that I can function.

One little beer won't hurt, right?

TWENTY-NINE

KATIE

I rub my forehead, my eyes still shut.

The pounding across my skull is unrelenting, and my mind is foggy.

I remember stopping outside the bar, and then... nothing.

Blank, once again. Nothing but a black void in my mind, a void now filled with the nauseating pulsing of a hangover. I let out a weary breath.

I guess it's fair to assume I went into the bar, then. My head shakes as I sit up in bed.

Why am I so weak? At the smallest inconvenience, it's like my entire body cries out for alcohol as the only possible solution.

As I move the covers off of me, I see that I'm still wearing last night's clothes and shoes. Wonderful. The bottom of my sheets are caked in dried dirt and street grime thanks to my soles.

My fingers have some weird pink dust on them. Actually, it's more like sand. I rub my index finger and thumb together, watching the pink sand fall from my hand with a dull mind.

I can't even begin to speculate what this is from. As I rotate my legs to get them onto the floor, my entire body seems to ache. My eyes are shut tight as I let out a breath.

Now that my brain has started up again, the questions of last night begin to return. Questions about Judith's guilt—and mine.

Despite feeling like a shell of a human physically, I'm actually able to quell my fear, somehow. Maybe it's the daylight. Light shed on dark thoughts always seems to lessen the severity of them.

Yes, it is still a horrifying possibility that I did murder Mark and frame Judith, all while not remembering any of it.

But now that I'm thinking more rationally about it, I'm able to consider a couple other facts. The police searched my place, too—and found absolutely nothing.

Wouldn't there have been something to find here, if I'd done it?

It wasn't like I was scheming to hide anything, as I didn't even know Mark was missing until the police told me.

Armed with that reminder, I'm able to take a small breath, and get a lid on the worst of the thoughts. With that issue tabled, my mind shifts again to Judith. What she said—or at least, tried to say, but I wouldn't hear it.

Even after our acrid exchange, guilt still bubbles up inside me. My younger sister might've been trying to tell me something, but I didn't let her.

My heart begins to beat a little faster. Could it really

be possible? Could Judith have been framed by someone else?

I was pissed at her yesterday. Obviously, she felt the same about me. Nothing new there.

But her life is on the line here. Despite everything that's passed between us, it makes my stomach twist a little.

My younger sister is in jail for killing Mark. My baby sister. As much animosity as I feel toward her right now, she is still my sister. We spent years of our lives as best friends.

Can *that* girl really be a monster?

My heart screams no, even as the evidence I've read about has my mind nodding to the contrary.

But what do I believe, deep down?

I swallow. Maybe I need to be the bigger person and go back to the jail. I am the big sister, after all.

Even though we hate each other right now, I think I owe it to Judith to at least hear her out. Then I can decide.

She might not even allow me to see her again, given how our conversation ended yesterday. But that's my baby sister in there, no matter what we said to each other.

THE BUZZING of the door lets me know Judith will soon appear. Surprisingly, she did agree to speak with me again. I shift my position on the rough plastic chair as I wait.

My entire body is tense. I'm thinking about so many

things right now—Mark, my fight with Judith, our relationship to each other.

It's a lot to deal with, but here I am.

Judith approaches the chair on the other side of the thick glass, her expression tough to read. She's always been that way, maintaining a look that's slightly distant and detached.

Now though, I really don't know what to make of it. Is it resignation, cold-bloodedness, or residual anger?

She takes her seat slowly, our eyes meeting as she lowers herself down. I chew on my lip and then reach for the phone. Judith does the same.

"Hey," I start, unsure really of what to say.

Judith is silent for a moment but then opens her mouth.

"Hey."

It comes out quietly. Does she feel the same way I do about how we left things yesterday?

My tongue moves across my dry lips. "Listen... I know we hate each other and everything right now, but... I can't stop thinking about what you tried to say yesterday. So if you say you didn't do it... I'll believe you."

Judith remains silent, watching me with the phone against her ear. Then her eyes begin to fill with tears.

"I'm your big sister, forever and always. No matter how screwed up I am—or you are," I continue, feeling my own face begin to warm as tears prick at my eyes.

A tear falls and rolls down Judith's cheek as I finish speaking. As our gazes meet again, I see her face has transformed.

Gone is the blank mask—the outer shield. Judith's lip trembles in a show of emotion I rarely see from her.

"I didn't do it, Katie," she says in a voice barely above a whisper.

A tearful laugh escapes my mouth as I let out a rush of air. She didn't do it.

My baby sister says she didn't kill Mark, and I don't care what everyone else says. She did not do it.

I'm nodding now as the tears continue to fall. "I believe you. I believe you, Judith."

She smiles now too, a look of relief washing over her face. Somehow, it's as if years of animosity between us have instantly fallen like a demolished building collapsing in on itself.

Sitting across from me is my sister, and I believe her. I'll always believe her, no matter what we say or do.

"I know how bad it looks," Judith says with a nod, "but I can explain."

"Yes, I followed Mark into the park that day—but only because I'd found out he was cheating on me, and didn't trust a word out of his mouth anymore."

"I didn't tell the police that because of how bad it looked. The only reason I don't appear on any camera leaving is that when I got to his father's bench, Mark wasn't there, so I tried finding him," she continues.

"I went out a different way, one of the smaller exits, one with not enough cameras I guess."

"And the ring?" I ask.

Judith shakes her head. "I have no idea how that got in there. But that's my daily purse that I carry all the time. Anyone passing me on the street could've dropped it in, and I'd have absolutely zero idea."

I nod, my cheek moving up and down against the receiver. It makes sense. And Judith is right—literally anyone could've planted it on her.

The bloody ring is the most damning piece of evidence against her. Really, it's the only evidence, but coupled with the camera feed and the email Mark wrote, it looks pretty ironclad.

But Judith is telling me she didn't do it, and I believe her. So if she didn't kill Mark, who did?

Judith seems to sense my thoughts. "I've been wracking my brain trying to figure out who could've done this, and why."

"And really, I just keep coming back to one person. Mia," she finishes.

I blink. "Mia?"

"Amelia's teacher. Mark and Mia were having an affair, and I found out. It's why it was so hard for me to be concerned about Mark when I first found out he was missing. You know my one-strike-and-you're-out policy. For all I knew, he'd spent the night at her place."

I nod again. Judith has always held very high standards for herself and those around her. Make a mistake, and you're done. Something I've experienced firsthand.

Very black-and-white thinking, but it's served her well enough. Until now, of course.

But as she speaks, I can see it in my mind. The media loves to harp on how unbothered Judith seemed by Mark's disappearance, and how any concern she showed seemed manufactured.

But they don't know her like I know her.

Mark messed up, and that meant he was dead to her. It's just the way she is, for better or worse.

But Mia. The schoolteacher. I think back to when I stumbled into the school and saw Mark talking with the young blonde-haired woman.

Thinking back on it, they were standing quite close to each other and separated rather quickly when I showed up.

"I think maybe Mia got jealous of Mark and me. Maybe he told her he wouldn't divorce me, or something. Either way, she wanted both of us to pay," Judith says.

And pay they have.

"But get this... the day Mark disappeared, I dropped Amelia off at school. Mia wasn't there. Apparently she had taken the day off," Judith says.

My mouth practically drops open.

Suddenly I feel as though I've been shocked by electricity as a thought rockets through me. I lean forward, my heart pumping.

"Wait a minute—two days ago, Doris said Mia came by her house to drop off schoolwork for Amelia. She also said Mia was talking about leaving the city. For good."

Judith's eyes widen as she and I come to the same conclusion. Mia is going to run. If she does, there's no way I'll be able to prove she's the real murderer.

My heart leaps up into my throat. Once Mia leaves NYC, it's over. Judith goes down for a crime she didn't commit.

I need to talk to Mia before she's gone. For all I know, she could be leaving right now or be gone already.

"I've got to find her, try and talk with her, see if I can get her to admit to something," I say, my eyes darting back and forth.

"It's a weekday, so try the school. If she's not there, I have her address."

I glance up at her sharply. Judith shrugs.

"She was messing around with my husband. I don't go into battle without accurate intel."

Despite everything that's happened, I can't help but crack a wry smile. Judith is Judith, all the way through.

After she gives me the address and I copy it into my phone, it's time to go.

If Mia told Doris she was leaving soon a couple days ago, soon could mean today. There isn't a minute to spare. I start stuffing my phone back into my pocket as I stand up from my chair.

"Katie," Judith says, pulling my attention back to her.

"No matter what happens... thank you. Thank you for coming back. I need my big sister right now," she says, her eyes glistening, "And I'm so sorry about everything I said."

Raising my hand, I put it up against the glass.

"That's what sisters are for. We're here for each other no matter what," I reply.

Judith matches my hand on the other side. Though we aren't touching each other physically, a wonderful flood of warmth moves through me as our palms align.

I've found my sister again.

I hold her gaze through the scratched glass. "I'm going to fix this, Judith. I swear I will."

She nods, still teary-eyed as I return the phone to its

place on the wall. Even after I pull my hand away from the glass, hers remains a few moments longer.

It's hard to make myself move away from her now that we've finally reconnected. But there's no time to waste.

If I don't do something, Judith is going to be convicted of a murder she didn't commit.

The police think they've found their culprit. The public does too. The thing is—Judith is my sister. My baby sister, and I believe her.

So while everyone else has already closed this case, I haven't.

That means I've got a murderous kindergarten teacher to talk to.

THIRTY
KATIE

I step out of the police precinct in a daze.

My mind is absolutely racing with things Judith said. Moving a mile a minute, working to pull the puzzle pieces together. It makes sense—almost too much sense.

How do the police not see this? They know Mia was in the picture.

The problem is the pile of evidence against Judith. And she had an obvious motive as far as they're concerned.

While we haven't exactly seen eye to eye as of late, she's still my sister. I may have failed her in the past, but I can't fail her now.

If there's ever a time to step up, this is it. Judith's very life may hang in the balance.

Out on the street, it takes me a few seconds to get my bearings. Beams of cold sunlight shine down through the scattered clouds overhead as the sidewalks bustle with activity. I descend into the chaos, picking at my nails with my fingertips.

There's just so much to think about as all the dots seem to come together.

Mia killed Mark and let Judith take the fall. The bloodied wedding ring, the smoking gun so to speak, was found in her purse—where Mia could've easily dropped it if she followed Judith on the street or maybe into a store where my sister would have been distracted.

All it would take is a second to plant the ring, and the case against Judith is ironclad.

The problem now is the police seem certain they have their suspect. I suppose in their eyes, given the overwhelming evidence, that's to be expected. But I can't agree.

Despite our differences, I believe Judith. I think she is innocent of killing Mark.

Now, I've just got to prove it. But how? All everyone knows right now is what Mia wants them to know. So far, her plan has worked perfectly.

I do a spin on the sidewalk, the buildings looming high around me.

The school isn't too far from here. I have to figure out the best way to confront her.

Maybe I should have my phone secretly recording in my pocket, and then ask her about Mark? Try to catch her off-guard, get her to admit what she's done.

I don't know if that would be enough to convict, but it's got to be something the police would want to look into, right?

That's all I need to do. Just get them to question what they think they know.

Legs pumping, I move with purpose down the streets

making my way to Amelia's school. There are several blocks between me and Bordley, but the time seems to move at warp speed in tune with my racing thoughts.

The whole way over, I'm trying to work out the best way to confront her. I've never done anything like this before, and now I'm starting to question the brazen approach.

If I start getting up into her face, she'll shut down, right?

Maybe instead I should act like I suspect her of nothing, and ask her to grab lunch on her break to talk about Amelia and how to support her during this difficult time.

Start to earn her trust and then see if I can work something out of her. That might be a better idea.

Another thought hits me and makes my stomach tighten a little. The last time Mia saw me it was when I was late picking up Amelia for school. Not exactly the best parental impression.

Taking a short breath, I duck my chin and keep walking. I won't let that deter me.

I've got to get something out of her. As I turn the corner, the school comes into view at the end of the street.

The red doors are open. I pick up my pace, heart beating faster and faster as I approach the school.

I've got to be really sure about this. I'm about to launch my own private investigation into a woman I don't know to try to prove she murdered my husband and framed my sister for it.

As I approach the wide steps, I take a final few

moments to think over my conversation with Judith one last time.

Do I truly believe her? Or am I just clinging onto any shred of hope that my sister is not some crazed psychopath?

It doesn't take long to find my answer. I trust my sister. We may not be best friends at this point in our lives, but she'll always be my sister. And when she says she didn't do it, I believe her.

The red doors are just a few steps away. I reach them and hustle up the three steps into the lobby of the school building.

A few kids dart around me in their uniforms, headed off to buy lunch. I make a beeline for the receptionist's window.

The foggy glass is shut, so I tap on it with my knuckles. My weight moves from foot to foot as I wait for the receptionist to open the window.

There's a squeak, and then she does.

"Hello," she says., "How can I help you?"

I lick my lips anxiously. "Yes, I'm looking to speak with Mia Goodridge, please."

My hand taps on the narrow counter beneath the window. I'm expecting the receptionist to maybe pick up her phone, but she starts shaking her head.

"I'm sorry. Ms. Goodridge is no longer a teacher here," she says.

My eyebrows draw together. "What do you mean, no longer teaching here? She's my daughter's kindergarten teacher."

My heart pounds heavily against my chest wall.

"Ms. Goodridge has resigned, effective immediately," the woman replies.

THIRTY-ONE
KATIE

My lungs burn as I run down the length of the street toward the subway station.

This can't be happening. Mia resigning from her job can only mean one thing—she's making a run for it.

I don't know how she could've figured out we were onto her, when we only just today put two and two together.

Maybe it has nothing to do with us. Maybe the police came to question her, or something.

If she was involved with Mark, there were probably text messages exchanged between the two of them, so she'd have been on their radar.

Whatever it is, she's been spooked. Leaving town "soon" has become *today*.

And if she leaves, that's it. Judith takes the fall, and Mia gets away scot-free.

I can't let it happen. My only hope is that she hasn't left the city yet.

I'm racing toward her apartment, my thoughts

hammering inside my skull. I don't know what I'm going to do if I get there and she's already gone.

That would be it—she'd be in the wind, and it'd be over.

She can't be. Not yet. Please.

I take the steps into the subway two at a time, my heart in my throat.

No train.

My foot taps anxiously as I wait in the underground station for the train to come. There's a cracked screen beside me that says the train should be here in five minutes. Five minutes too long.

I picture Mia in my mind, stuffing her suitcases and cleaning out her apartment. For all I know, these five minutes could be the difference between Judith being found guilty or not.

She has to still be there.

Finally the train comes, and I shuffle into it with the rest of humanity. We're packed in here like cattle, all of us pressed up against each other's puffy coats and jackets.

As soon as the doors shut, I break out into a sweat. Squished in here like this, with all the layers I'm wearing, and given the situation, I'm feeling like I might pass out from heat stroke.

My fingers fumble for the zipper of my jacket as the train rocks back and forth over the tracks.

We slide into the next stop, screeching to a halt. It takes an agonizingly long time for the doors to open and people to pile out and in.

We *need* to start moving again, now. Right this

instant, because there is a murderer on the loose, and she's going to get away.

I'm a sweat-streaked mess by the time we reach the stop nearest Mia's apartment. I can feel the beads of perspiration running down the length of my torso as I push through the crowded car toward the door.

"Excuse me," I say, working my way through.

I just manage to slip out before the doors close behind me. I don't wait to catch my breath, taking off for the staircase the second I get free.

When I emerge from the station, the blast of cold wind above ground makes me gasp, but I appreciate it after baking in that subway car. The chill sharpens my mind, allowing me to get over the chaos of my thoughts for a moment.

My hand trembles slightly as I pick up my phone and consult it to figure out which direction I'm supposed to walk in. Left. I need to go left.

Cutting through the crowd, I'm jogging again as I cross the street.

A car honks from somewhere behind me, but I don't turn around. I just need to get to Mia's before it's too late.

All the way there, a cruel voice whispers that I'm already too late. That she's already gotten away with murder.

I recognize it. It's the same voice that whispers temptation for me to have a drink whenever things feel hard.

This time, I manage to shut it down, physically shaking my head back and forth as I break into a trot.

Almost there. Two more blocks, and then I'll be at her building.

There are fewer people on the sidewalks now, allowing me to pick up the pace to a flat-out run that has my lungs burning from the cold oxygen reaching them.

My nose is running, too. I sniffle hard and swipe my jacket arm underneath it to try and wipe some of the moisture away. Gross, but there's no time for fancy manners here.

I'm only a block away now, and that gives me the energy to push my tired legs just a little bit harder.

When I reach her block, I look left and right for the building. There. I cross the street and come up to it, lungs absolutely burning. I'm practically doubled over in the doorway as I scan the console built into the wall.

Apartment eleven. That's her. I mash down the call button with my thumb as I gasp for oxygen. Nothing happens.

My throat tightens as my ribs ache. *No. Please.*

I press down on the button again, hard. Still no answer. Is it because she doesn't want to answer, or because she's already left?

My fearful thoughts threaten to crush me. *I'm too late. It's over.*

Stumbling backwards, I come up against the other side of the doorway with my back as I suck in air and try to focus.

I see my sister's tears in my mind again. Then I see Amelia.

If I can't fix this, she'll grow up hearing that Judith killed her father. My eyes snap back open, and I go to the console again.

This time, I press the buttons for every single apartment. Someone has to let me in.

"Come on," I say through gritted teeth. "Please–please–please."

Then the door buzzes. Unlocked. Someone buzzed me in. Not sure who, don't care.

I push against the door, and then I'm inside, shoes squeaking on the tile floor. Rushing to the staircase, I look up at the spiral of stairs, breathing hard from running. I haven't exactly been working out lately.

No time to catch my breath now. These are the final moments.

Apartment eleven is on one of the upper floors, maybe two or three. So up I go, taking the steps as quickly as I can manage them.

In a matter of seconds, I'll find out if Mia's already fled. If I'm already too late.

If so, this whole mad dash will have been for naught —but I've got to try. My legs are on fire as I climb the staircase, feeling rubbery and weak after my sprint from the subway.

I can't give in. I need to know.

Reaching the second floor, I peer down the hallway at the door numbers. No eleven. Back to the stairs.

This is it. Last flight. I grab hold of the bannister and practically drag myself up to the third floor and onto the landing, my head whipping left and right.

And then I see it—apartment eleven, just off to my left.

That's not all I see.

The door is ajar, *and I can hear Mia inside.*

THIRTY-TWO

KATIE

I freeze, my feet pinned to the hallway floor as I stare at the open door.

I swear that noise came from inside. Am I just imagining things?

The door is a couple steps off to my right. Easing closer to it, I listen as hard as I can for any other sounds specifically from apartment eleven.

Nothing reaches me. It's quiet again, making me think whatever I heard must have come from one of the other apartments.

My spirits crash, all of the adrenaline I built up on the run over here sinking down to—

There. I *definitely* heard something from inside, no doubt about it this time. My heart climbs up my throat as my head snaps back up, eyes locked on the door.

Some sort of rustling again. Instantly my mouth goes dry. *She's still in there.*

I'm not too late—I'm right on time.

My fingers tingle as I remain standing in the hallway,

completely unsure of what's supposed to come next. I ran all the way over here to confront her, but I think part of me didn't truly expect to get this far.

But I'm here now, and she's in there. I need to do something, right now.

I take another step toward the door, placing my sneaker down as quietly as I can. My entire body is tensed as I try and stay alert for any sound or movement in the apartment.

There are more noises. Impossible to tell from my location out here in the hall what she's doing in there, but one thing's for sure—Mia's definitely home.

Now what?

There isn't any air left in my lungs to breathe out. All that separates me from a murderer is six inches of wood door.

What will happen to me if I make my presence known?

What will happen if I *don't* and just allow her to slip away, unchallenged?

I think again of Judith and the tears in her eyes as she looked at me through the glass barrier at the jail. She needs me. My sister needs me.

It's hard to swallow. I'm only allowing myself to breathe through my nose, even though my lungs still burn from all the exertion. I'm doing everything I can to control my breathing so I don't give myself away.

Swallowing my terror, I straighten myself up and raise a hand to knock on the door.

My knuckles come down against the wood, harder than I meant them to. The force of my knock sways the door slightly inward, revealing a sliver of the interior of Mia's apartment. The first thing I notice is the walls— they're a musty yellow.

"Mia, it's Katie," I say, then add, "Amelia's mother. I know you're in there."

The apartment has fallen quiet again. Maybe alerting Mia to my presence was the wrong move.

The more I think about it, the more certain I am of it. I should've never told a killer I was right outside. *I'm so bad at this.*

My mind creates an image of Mia crouched inside in the dark, fingers closing around the hilt of a sharp butcher's knife as she slinks toward the door.

But then ten seconds pass, and I'm still alive. Mia isn't screaming or attacking me. In fact, there's nothing but total silence.

Is she hoping I'll just give up and walk away?

I've already heard her inside. I know she's in there. There's quite literally zero chance I'm leaving here until I get some answers.

My hand digs into the pocket of my jacket, looking for anything I might use to defend myself. All I find is a metal bottle cap opener. It's been in there for years.

It'll have to do, because I'm not going away.

Still no response from inside. Now I'm starting to wonder. If Mia is so dangerous, why hasn't she attacked me yet?

Or at the very least, run up and shut the door?

And if she has nothing to hide—or pretending to— why wouldn't she have answered my knock or my call? Why isn't she standing in front of me right now, demanding to know why I'm here, or how I know where she lives?

There's just nothing. My throat closes a little as a new thought hits me.

Is she even home at all? Or am I talking to a rat or cockroach inside?

"Mia?" I ask again.

My voice sounds much too loud in the silence of the hallway. Somewhere above me something thuds, making me tense up, but it's not coming from Mia's apartment.

Distantly I hear a siren as an ambulance responds to one of the city's never-ending emergencies.

Mia still hasn't answered me. The crushing thoughts of being too late are once again threatening to take over my mind. They make my knees feel weak.

My sister spending the rest of her natural life in prison, convicted of a murder she didn't commit.

My daughter having to grow up never really knowing the truth about her father.

The nightmare scenarios threaten to derail my mind completely, my thoughts beginning to skitter out of control. I push against the door in a last-ditch effort to save my own sanity. I have to know.

The door lets out a squeak as it swings open all the way. The apartment is dark, save for the weak gray sunlight that illuminates part of the main room from a window somewhere out of sight.

The rest of the apartment is cast in shadow. My thoughts shift back to those images of Mia crouched in the darkness, just waiting for me to take another step.

In a flash of brutal movement, I'm dead.

Licking my lips, I call out Mia's name again. It's not a large apartment, only a single hallway that leads into the studio bedroom. Off to my left is what looks like a door to the bathroom, but it's shut.

My chest squeezes so tight I can hardly breathe as I take another step inside, one hand clutching the bottle opener as the other reaches toward the bathroom door.

I throw it open with an involuntary shout, my entire body feeling like a live wire. Even in the dark however, it's clear there's no Mia in here. Just a small toilet and shower with its curtain pushed to the side.

Stepping out again, I scan the walls on both sides for a light switch. There—across from me. Crossing the hall to it, I flick it up with bated breath.

A harsh yellow light cuts through the darkness like a blade, making my eyes burn for a moment as I stand there in the hallway.

Looking ahead, I can now clearly make out the small desk in front of me, pushed against the far wall. A desk chair is tucked neatly underneath it. Shelves hang on the wall above it. A little closer to me is a TV monitor on a small dresser about knee-height.

My legs carry me forward as I creep further into the apartment, the opener held up like a weapon.

Just as I'm about to reach the end of the short hallway and enter into the main area, there's another noise.

Whirling to my left, my hand comes up defensively as my eyes snap wide—only to see the actual source of the noises I heard.

The window in front of me is open. As the wind

gusts through it, the curtain moves, slapping the empty water bottles on the table beside the bed.

The bottle opener lowers. This whole time, I've been prepping for a battle with the wind.

As the anti-climactic discovery washes over me, so does the truth.

I really am too late. There's no one here.

Mia left in such a hurry she left the window and door open. Maybe I just missed her. My stomach twists into a knot.

What if in my haste to get here, I ran right past her on the street? She easily could've been one of the people I knocked into and didn't bother to look at.

I'm trying to rack my brain, conjuring up brief flashes of faces as I ran by, but it does no good.

Either way, Mia is gone. So too are any chances of getting the truth. My shoulders slump downward as I fight back tears.

What am I going to tell Judith? Once again, I've failed her.

Something on the bed draws my attention, and makes my breath catch in my throat.

A dot of red. Another gust of wind rolls through from my left as I take a real look at the bed for the first time since entering the apartment.

As I do, I notice that the sheets appear to have been partially yanked off and over to the other side.

The side I can't see right now. Blinking, I slowly walk toward the bed, my eyes landing on more drops of red standing out against the white bed sheets. They're twisting like snakes off the mattress, disappearing out of sight.

My heart beats faster, my pulse pounding like a drum in my head as I round the bed.

A horn honks outside, but I can't look away. I need to find out what's on the other side of the bed.

I almost wish that I hadn't, because as Mia's dead body comes into view, everything begins to spiral.

THIRTY-THREE

KATIE

I can't breathe.

I stumble backward, a scream caught in my closed throat as I crash into the air conditioner unit behind me and lose my footing, landing on my rear.

Mia's body is twisted up in the bed sheets, her eyes wide and mouth open as she stares lifelessly at the ceiling overhead. Her blonde hair is spattered with blood.

Blood is everywhere. It spreads out around her, coating the floor and soaking into the sheets. All across her chest and legs, there are splotches of red.

There's zero question as to whether she's still alive or not. She's been murdered, stabbed.

Digging my heels into the floor in front of me, I scoot away. My back comes up against the desk chair, making me shriek.

I can't look away from Mia. She's dead, and none of this makes any sense whatsoever.

My thoughts are a jumbled mess, all of them

screaming at once for my attention as I work to try and pull myself together.

What happened here?

Somebody killed Mia obviously, but *she's* supposed to be the murderer.

My ragged breathing isn't getting enough oxygen into my system. I feel light-headed, nauseous. Reaching up a hand, I manage to grab the edge of the desk and pull myself back to a standing position. I lean against the desk, trying to breathe, trying to think.

None of this makes any sense. My rapid glances around the room reveal nothing except the empty kitchen area and the open window. The pounding of my pulse in my head is so loud I can't even think. If only I...

My entire body freezes as my gaze falls to the desk I'm up against. More specifically, what sits on top of the desk.

Just behind me is a small zen garden box. In it is a miniature rake, and some balls.

But that isn't what sends my mind into complete and utter delirium.

It's the *pink sand* that fills the box. The same sand I found on my hands this morning.

THIRTY-FOUR
KATIE

This can't be happening. This isn't real.

My vision quakes as I stare down at the sand, my entire body humming. There is nothing else but the pulsing inside my head as I reach forward with a shaking hand.

Pink sand. Just like the mysterious substance I found on my hand and in my bed this morning.

I don't remember going to bed last night. I woke up this morning exhausted. I can't breathe.

My fingers come closer to the sand box. The innocent pink color of the sand completely juxtaposes the crushing feelings of guilt that are completely overriding my system.

It's not possible. It can't be.

I place a finger into the sandbox. As I do, I feel something. My vision flickers. There's something in here, tucked beneath the sand.

My knees threaten to give out as my heart squeezes so tight it's physically painful.

My fingers close around the object and lift it from the pastel-colored sand. As they do, the last bit of my sanity gives way.

In my hand is a boxcutter. *My* boxcutter. The one I couldn't find earlier when I wanted to cut my jeans off. Blood is caked onto the silver blade of the knife, grains of pink sand covering it like a dusting of snow.

Sand falls from my hand as my vision flickers again. Then I'm in the desk chair—my legs have given out completely. The boxcutter clatters to the floor, and everything begins to spin.

All at once, the truth hits me like a truck. The horrible, awful truth.

Mia never did anything to Mark. Neither did Judith. *I* did.

I think back to waking up with dirt under my nails the morning after Mark disappeared. I knew where he was going to be. It was the day his Dad died, which meant he would be in Central Park at the bench.

Central Park, just about the only place in the city with real dirt.

I'd been to the bench before. Mark took me there once.

I had motive, too. He was taking away Amelia. To drunk me, that was too much to bear.

I remember nothing. Just the guilt the next morning, and the total lack of memories.

All of this floods my system at once, like some information download from a phantom wire jammed directly into my brain.

All of it fits. Judith's arrest. Even sober, I've stalked her and Mark.

Completely blacked out, I must have planted the ring in her purse.

Because I didn't remember anything, I was able to obscure my guilt from the police.

My eyes move back over to Mia's body lying beside the bed. Judith told me about Mia and Mark, but I must've already known. I'd seen them standing so close when I went to pick up Amelia.

Another thunderbolt strikes me as I finally realize this woman is the same woman I saw outside Mark's apartment the night after they went upstate.

I saw their conversation from across the street.

Again, drunk me wouldn't stand for it.

I'm a monster. A Jekyll and Hyde, capable of humanity only in the daylight hours. What comes out at night is something else entirely.

I could never control my drinking. Who I become when I drink is uncontrollable and apparently violent.

Hot flashes move across my body as the reality of what I've done sets in.

I killed Mark. I murdered him. Me.

I killed the father of my child, but that wasn't enough. I slaughtered my daughter's schoolteacher, too.

The fact that all of it was done in a drunken rage doesn't matter. That's no excuse—certainly not to a jury.

I am a killer. An uncontrollable monster who needs to be stopped.

I'm on my feet again. I don't know exactly when that happened. Nothing feels real as I stagger for the door.

I can't keep going like this. Now that I know the truth, it needs to end. Who knows who else I'm going to hurt.

Judith was never the killer sister. I was. This whole time, I've been allowing myself to believe it couldn't have been me. I was all too happy to let her take the blame, because it absolved me of any dark wonderings that might've taken root in me. What-if questions that I had no answers for.

Now I do. Now I see the truth.

I'm back in the hallway, stumbling down the steps. I careen into the wall and right myself again. I am a dangerous person, capable of anything.

I can't be allowed to drink anymore.

Two people are dead because of me.

The back of my hand runs across my mouth. I need to call the police with the last few shreds of my rational mind. Tell them what I've done before I hurt anyone else.

But if I do that, I'll never see her again. I'll never see my beautiful daughter again.

That sends a spike of pain through my stomach so agonizing I wince, stopping my descent to lean against the wall as tears pour down my cheeks.

It's over. My life is over. And it's because of me. All because of me.

I see Mark in my mind as my body propels me forward. He hugs me, grinning as we laugh together and fall off the couch and onto the floor. I'd just told him we'd be having a kid.

All he wanted was to be a father. He never got to

know his dad, and was determined he wouldn't let the same happen to his child.

I un-made that decision for him.

Mark holding baby Amelia, eyes filled with tears as he looked at her for the first time. He called her perfect.

Because of me, Amelia will never get to spend another second with her father.

I'm out on the street now. My shattered mind moves to the liquor bottle on the counter. The voice in my head as it called to me.

The next day, Mark was gone. Buried somewhere in Central Park. I have to remember, but I can't.

When I blink again, I'm standing outside Doris's house. What am I doing here?

My daughter. I need to see her one last time. Need to hold her.

I feel feverish. My arms wrap around her, squeezing her tight, but I open my eyes, and she's not here. The ache in my chest is overwhelming. I'm at the door.

Numbly, my finger comes up to press down on the doorbell. It doesn't even feel like my own arm that does it. The buzz echoes through my mind.

I just need to see her. That's it. Hold her one last time before everything changes. My baby girl. More tears roll down my face as I press the doorbell again.

"Coming," I hear from inside.

"Who is it, Gammie?" Amelia shouts, her voice slightly muffled by the wall between us.

Sounds like she's on the upper floor. Just the sound of her voice makes me cry even harder. I just need to see my baby.

"It's me," I shout, my voice breaking.

"Please open the door."

The locks turn in the door as the sound of footsteps thudding on the stairs fills my ears. Then the door opens, Doris standing in the opening. Her eyes are wide as she looks me up and down.

"What's going on?" she asks.

"Is that Mommy?" I hear Amelia say from somewhere behind her.

She's just out of my field of vision, still on the staircase. I crane my neck but can't see her. I just want to see her—why can't I see her?

"Just a second honey," Doris calls over her shoulder.

To me she says, "You shouldn't have come here, looking like that."

There's a note of alarm in her voice that pulls me back. Then I look down at myself and see why. Spots of blood dot my jeans and shirt. Mia's blood.

I look like an absolute mess. Covered in sweat, bloodstains down my jean legs. I don't care—I want to see my daughter.

My hands grip onto the cold metal bars of the outer door as I come up against it.

"Doris, let me in," I say.

"Katie, what's going on? What happened?" she asks, bewildered.

"Mommy?" Amelia calls, making me even more manic.

"Baby it's me," I say, smiling even while the tears keep coming.

"Mommy is here."

Amelia bounds down the rest of the steps, smiling, though her expression changes to worry the moment she gets a look at me.

"Mommy what's wrong?"

I desperately need to hold her.

"Doris, please open the door, okay?"

Doris nods and unlocks it, and finally I'm allowed inside. She's asking me if I'm okay I think, but I can't hear her. Everything else melts away as I pull Amelia into a hug.

My eyes shut tight as I squeeze her, and for just a moment, all is right in the world.

But then everything comes crashing back into my mind, and I drag my eyelids open again.

"Katie, what happened? What is going *on*?" Doris asks.

Letting out a breath, I force myself to let go of Amelia. She's looking up at me with far too much concern than a five-year-old should ever feel. My hand runs under my nose. I think I'm on the verge of a total breakdown.

"Mommy are you okay?" Amelia asks, looking up at me.

I smile down at her and nod. "Of course, baby. Just so excited to see you, that's all."

My thoughts roar in my head. I don't want her around for this, when they take me away. Her last memory of me should be something good.

My eyes find Doris's, who seems to sense there is something to discuss that Amelia should not be present for.

"Honey, Mommy needs a minute, and then we'll all head next door," she says. "Why don't you and I go over now and let Mommy get settled for a minute? You can play with Tommy."

Doris does her best to give Amelia a bright smile, and after a moment, my daughter nods.

They both put on their coats.

"Ruby's grandson is here for Thanksgiving break," Doris explains to me.

I can only nod silently, biting back the surge of tears that threaten to overtake me. I'm suddenly aware of the fact that these are some of the last few seconds I will ever spend looking at my daughter.

Amelia is oblivious to it all, slipping into her puffy coat as she jumps around with excitement at seeing the boy next door.

"You're gonna help us bake again, right Mommy?" Amelia asks.

I nod, my eyes misty. "Of course I am, baby. I'll be right over."

Amelia smiles and heads out the front door with Doris. It pains me everywhere in my entire body to see her go, but I can't have her around when I tell Doris everything.

"I love you," I call through the open doorway in a choked voice. Amelia's already racing toward the gate at the end of the driveway.

My vision flickers slightly as the door closes all the way and I can't see her anymore. But I made a promise to myself. I saw her one last time, and now it's over.

I land hard in a chair at the kitchen table and just sit there with my eyes shut as I wait for Doris to return. Even in darkness, the world seems to spin. I hear the front door open again, and then Doris strides into the kitchen.

"Okay Katie, *what* is going on? Why are you covered in blood? You're scaring me," she says.

This is it. I got to see Amelia one last time, and now I owe it to Mark and Mia and everyone else I've ever hurt to put a stop to this.

It has to end. I let out a long breath and look over at her.

Doris looks at me expectantly as she reaches for the tea kettle on top of the stove.

"Doris... I... I killed Mark," I say.

It doesn't seem to really register on her face. Only after a second do her eyebrows pull together, and she starts to shake her head.

"What?"

I nod. Now that I've started, I can't stop. I tell her about the blacking out and waking up with dirt under my nails. I tell her about not remembering anything.

I tell her about stalking my sister and Mark. I tell her about going to Mia's apartment and finding out that I'd already been there during another blackout.

"All of it was me. I did it, not Judith," I finish.

Doris stares at me, her face pale. Her hand is still frozen on the tea kettle.

"I know it will do nothing. I know it's too late. But I want you to know I'm sorry. I'm so, so sorry," I say, my eyes tearing up again.

"Call the police and tell them I'm here," I say, my eyes shutting as I rub my face, "and it'll all be over."

Doris is shaking her head, not looking at me.

"You shouldn't have come here," she says again, her voice barely above a whisper.

The movie playing downstairs is muffled by the floorboards. I nod, biting my lip.

"I know. I know. I'm sorry– I just... I needed to see her. And... I guess I wanted you to know the truth. From me. I'm sorry."

"No, you don't understand. You weren't *supposed* to come here," Doris says, her head shaking harder.

I lift my eyes to her, confused. When I do, I only catch sight of the knife in her hand at the last second.

THIRTY-FIVE
KATIE

The chair legs screech across the floorboards as I jump up and out of the reach of the blade sweeping toward me.

"What are you doing?" I ask breathlessly, stumbling back away from the kitchen table.

"You don't have to be afraid of me. I would never hurt you," I assure her. "I want to turn myself in."

Doris stands in front of me, her jaw tight and her shoulders rising and falling. She points the knife toward me. The tip of it shines with reflected light from the overhead fixture.

My bewildered gaze flicks around the room. What is going on? Does Doris really think I'd attack her after I've just confessed?

"You were supposed to turn yourself in at the station, not bring the police *here*," Doris hisses.

I stare at her, trying to wrap my head around this. I still have absolutely no idea what's going on—one second I'm sitting next to my ex-mother-in-law, and now she's just tried to kill me.

"What—" I start, but Doris's step forward cuts me off.

"Judith was supposed to go down for Mark, and you for that teacher, Mia," she says.

I can't pull my eyes away from the sharp glint of the knife clutched in her hand. Then her words finally resonate with me, and my head snaps up.

Wait a minute...

The way she's speaking, it's like all of this was planned. That it was some sort of set-up. Does that mean...

Did I *not* kill Mark and Mia? Could that really be true?

I want to believe it, but even now, there are so many facts that seem to point to me.

"But... the blackouts," I say, my mind racing, "the dirt and sand. My boxcutter."

Doris looks at me, her jaw clenched. She's not defending herself. She's not contradicting me either.

"You... *you're* the killer?" I ask, the words tumbling out of me breathlessly.

Doris still says nothing, but I can tell from her expression I've finally arrived at the truth.

It feels like my brain is shattering.

Over and over during this whole thing I've felt like I've finally found the answer, only to have the rug pulled out from under me. The puzzle nearly completed, and yet just as I go to place the last piece, the entire puzzle changes once more.

I don't know how or why, but Doris orchestrated everything.

She killed Mark and framed Judith for it, planting the ring in her purse. Then she killed Mia and framed me.

Somehow.

For some reason, but—

A horrible thought strikes me. The boxcutter missing from my apartment when I went looking for it the other day. It wasn't because I had forgotten where I placed it... it was because *Doris had been inside my apartment and took it.*

That means she must've forced the dirt and sand under my nails, too. But wouldn't I have woken up?

How could I sleep through something like that?

None of this feels real right now, and yet the knife in Doris's grip lets me know that somehow, some way, it is. This is not a dream.

"You're just like your father, you know that?" Doris snaps suddenly, her lips curled into a snarl.

The comment is so unexpected that it makes my hands lower slightly from their defensive position. Doris knew my father?

"A waste of a person like him," she spits, "ruining the lives of others and facing no consequences. Well, not anymore."

The words sting, but only until the knife comes back up, and then it's all I can focus on.

I can't spare the brainpower right now to process what she's saying or figure out how she knew my dad, alongside every other revelation that's hit me like a bus.

I stumble backwards, my back coming up against the kitchen wall. Only too late do I realize I've cornered myself with only the small round kitchen table separating us.

"Wait, please," I say desperately.

The doorway to the dining room is just to my left, but I don't know if I can reach it before Doris reaches me.

"If your father hadn't fired my John, he'd still be here today, do you realize that?" Doris says, her eyes welling up with angry tears.

John—Mark's Dad. Suddenly things are starting to make more sense. Doris apparently blames *us* for what our father did to her.

I lick my lips, putting my hands out in front of me.

"Doris—I get it. That's a terrible thing, my Dad firing your husband. He shouldn't have," I start, "but—"

"Your family *destroyed* mine," she growls, cutting me off. "I'm only returning the favor."

Tears stream down her face now, a vein pulsing on her forehead. The picture finally becomes clear in my mind. My father fired her husband, who committed suicide as a result. Doris was left with baby Mark and no way to earn income.

Now, she's making Judith and me pay.

All of it is horrible, incomprehensible... and yet here we are. In her twisted mind, this seems like justice.

I'm utterly exhausted mentally, but even still, there's one part of Doris' explanation that doesn't seem to add up.

My head shakes back and forth as my entire body trembles.

"But... if you wanted to get back at our family, why

kill Mark, too? He's your own son," I say, my voice trembling.

Doris lowers the knife slightly as her eyes shift to the dining room behind me.

"I never said I did," she says, a ghost of a smile on her face.

A creaking floorboard has me whirling around—and coming face-to-face with *Mark*.

His body fills up the doorway, alive and completely unharmed. My heart pounds as I stare, unable to comprehend what is happening.

"Hey Katie," he says simply.

It's the last thing I hear before he lunges at me.

PART 3

THIRTY-SIX
MARK

Being dead is harder work than I thought it would be.

No one can see me walking around obviously, which means Mom has to go out any time I need anything. My missing person's case got a *lot* more press than we were expecting, too, which made things even more challenging.

A couple of reporters even showed up here at the house during the first few days after the story broke. I could hear them trying to get a statement out of Mom from my hiding spot in the garage.

At first, we were worried all the extra attention might disrupt things, but it eventually settled down. This is New York City, after all.

Here, it's like the news tries to top itself. Every day, some new insanity seems to take place, stealing the spotlight from the previous atrocity.

Once Judith was arrested for my disappearance and murder, the public interest began to fade. Everyone had their satisfactory ending.

That made me feel more comfortable about going out occasionally, though of course only with a beanie, scarf, and sunglasses. And even then, I only left the garage when it was absolutely necessary.

To kill Mia, for instance.

I couldn't let my mother climb up that fire escape, not with her hip. I still feel bad about having to kill Mia, but Mom said it was the only way. An acceptable casualty, she called her.

So while I didn't love it, I went along with what she said, because that's what a good son does.

And I have been a good son. From the very beginning, when Mom first told me this was how we would get our revenge for what happened to Dad.

So when she showed me photos of Katie Rose and where she worked, I didn't hesitate.

It took a couple years, but eventually I got her to marry me. All according to the plan. The next step was pitting the sisters against each other.

I started injecting Katie with alcohol via syringe after about a year together. Mom, being a phlebotomist, showed me how to do it so the person doesn't even feel it —or so they don't even wake up.

Injecting alcohol intravenously bypasses the body's natural filtration system, leading to an immediate surge of alcohol into the bloodstream. Essentially, the person gets drunk almost instantaneously.

Given how much I was giving her, her body began to regularly crave more and more alcohol. From there it was easy—I just let Katie do all the work to destroy our marriage with her supposed sudden onset of alcoholism. Every time she'd black out, I'd take some more money from her inheritance and tell her she'd spent it gambling while drunk. Little by little, what was hers became mine, until the entirety of her two-million dollar inheritance belonged to Mom and me.

All the while, I played the supportive, caring husband. The man with the wife everyone knew was a mess.

It was around that time I started "opening up" to Judith. I'd always known she'd found me attractive, as Katie had told me on our first date that her sister was jealous.

I took my time with Judith, because she's very smart. It had to seem entirely natural that I began to fall for her through all this. She was there for me when her sister wasn't, after all.

Given how much I'd made Katie's body crave alcohol, it didn't take long for things to reach a point where I could reasonably divorce her after I'd siphoned all the money.

From there, it only took a couple nights spent crying at my apartment with Judith consoling me to win her over.

It might have seemed to her like that first kiss was spur of the moment, but of course everything was planned. In fact, Mom was hidden in the other room listening to every word, making sure it all went down the way we'd rehearsed.

The next couple of years were easy. After ensuring that our marital assets go to Amelia, I could sit back. Most of the heavy lifting had been done, and then it was just time to establish normal routines.

Of course, I still had to write up the threatening notes and send them to Judith and me, supposedly from Katie. Every note I sent seemed to make Judith hate her sister even more.

We didn't even plan to have Katie show up drunk to crash the wedding, that was just a happy accident. Mom and I couldn't have planned it any better.

So I played the role of Judith's husband, waiting for Mom to decide when we would make our next move. Parents know best, after all.

A few weeks back, when I was dropping off Amelia, Mom told me it was time. There was both excitement and a little bit of anxiety.

We'd started all this over six years ago at this point, so this was a long time in the making.

Talking about it, working through every little hypothetical. But here we were, actually about to go through with it.

Starting up the notes again was easy enough. Judith was so ready to blame her sister. It was fairly easy giving them both a reason to kill me, too.

The day I went missing was a big day. Everything had led up to this, and Mom was counting on me. For Dad. That's why we did it on the anniversary of his death —to honor him. Getting ahold of the sisters' inheritances didn't hurt in encouraging me to participate, either.

After nicking my finger and smearing some blood on my wedding ring, I slipped it into Judith's purse before she left with Amelia to drop her off.

Then I made sure to waltz into the park where I knew the cameras would see me. After that, I typed up that email draft blaming the Rose sisters, just like Mom had instructed.

Next stop was slipping out of the park, which was a little more challenging as I had to cut through the woods and hop over the wall at a place not meant to enter or exit.

Got it done, though. Mom was busy using the copied keys I made of Katie's building and front door to slip into her apartment and inject her with a massive dose of alcohol. Enough to make her black out and wonder what she'd done.

Then it was simple... dress her like she'd been out, cut her leg, and stuff dirt under her nails.

A perfect cocktail for a guilty conscience. Katie's always been quick to blame herself.

After that, all Mom had to do was dress up as a runner and "find" my phone in the park then give it to the first police officer she found.

From there, we knew it was only a matter of time before the police got into the phone and found the email draft. Hearing on the news that they called in Judith and Katie both made me smile. Soon, Judith would be arrested for my murder, and given a life sentence. As such, Mom would receive Power of Attorney over Judith's assets so she could care for Amelia–and get access to the rest of the Rose family fortune.

Everything was going exactly as we'd dreamed it.

The only part I didn't like was having to hold Mia hostage. Breaking into that apartment through the window the first time felt pretty bad, especially given how much I knew she liked me.

But Mom said it had to be done. Mia had to appear suspicious in the eyes of the Rose sisters, and so that meant making her call out of work immediately after my disappearance. I had her bound and gagged in her apartment for days, just waiting for the word.

Mom kept an eye on Katie after lying to her about Mia coming to the house and saying she was looking to skip town. When Katie met with Judith in the jail, we knew it was time.

The sisters thought they'd finally found the culprit.

I typed up an email on Mia's computer and had her resign. Killing her with the boxcutter Mom took from Katie's was upsetting, to say the least. Mom said it was what had to happen, though. So I did it. Like a good son.

We were too far into this to turn back now anyway.

While I was at Mia's, Mom was back in Katie's apartment injecting her once more. The final dose. After that, she got to work sprinkling pink sand from the bag I'd filled the last time I was in Mia's apartment.

It hasn't been easy since losing Dad. Mom says those first few years were almost unbearable. All the while though, she was plotting her revenge.

That's what I love about her—she really would do anything for those she loves.

So while it hasn't always been easy, we did it. And we were getting away with it.

Or at least, we *had*, until Katie showed up here unannounced.

That wasn't supposed to happen. After finding Mia

dead, she was supposed to go to the police station and turn herself in,taking all the blame.

Given the evidence presented to her and knowing her self-blame and guilty conscience, it was the only rational choice for her to make.

The entire Rose family would be ruined and my family would finally be as rich as we deserved to be.

Our revenge would finally be complete. Total victory.

But I forgot that Katie isn't like Judith. She isn't nearly as predictable.

Now we've got to operate on the fly, thanks to Katie's insistence on seeing Amelia.

What she doesn't understand is that Amelia is a part of my family, not hers. Me, Mom, and Amelia. The three of us together, happy.

I love my daughter, and I love my mother. I want the absolute best for them, even if Amelia still doesn't know I'm alive yet. I'm letting Mom handle all of that.

She can explain the family history much better than I can, explain why it's so important we have and trust only each other.

That's why Katie showing up is such a problem. If the cops come here and do any kind of a search, they'll realize pretty quickly I've been hiding out in the garage, very much not dead.

So as Katie pours out what she thinks is the truth to Mom, I sneak out of the garage and into the house again.

I will admit, the look on Katie's face as she realizes I'm still alive is priceless.

So is the one when I lunge toward her.

"I'll get her favorite kind. It's vodka, right?"

The words reach my ears, but I don't open my eyes. My cheek is pressed up against something hard—the floor.

I'm on the floor in the kitchen, Mark and Doris standing over me.

"Yeah. Are you sure you don't want me to come with you, Mom?"

"Stay here with her. We need to hurry. I'm expected next door. You injected her with the whole syringe, right?"

"Yeah. She was fighting pretty hard, but I got it in. She should be down for a while," Mark says.

I let out a low mumble from my place on the floor, my eyes closed.

The thing is—I'm not intoxicated. At all. I'm faking this entirely, pretending I've just been given a heavy dose of alcohol.

"Fine. I'll tell Amelia that Katie had to leave. Load

her into the car and then take her to her apartment and then inject her again—the vein this time—another one in the muscle, and it'll leave an obvious mark. That should be enough to end it," Doris says.

Mark rushed me with a needle. He got it into my arm, too—but I felt the needle break as I fought for my life. Twisting as hard as I was, the thin needle snapped off in my shoulder muscle, and the alcohol squirted out onto my arm, not in it.

The skin still feels damp on my arm, but I made sure to tuck it under my body when I collapsed so they wouldn't see.

All of it happened in a split-second. Even now, I'm fighting against my own body to curb the urge to hyperventilate, because if I do, they'll know my *dear* husband missed the target.

I've got to seem completely out of it, it's the only chance I have.

The floorboards squeak as Doris heads toward the front of the house. According to their conversation, she's going to the liquor store down the street to buy the brand of vodka I used to drink.

If they dump me off at my apartment and inject me again intravenously, it'll look like I just drank until I gave myself fatal alcohol poisoning. Knowing how thorough they are, she'll probably instruct Mark to pour half the bottle down my throat for good measure.

Given everything else, the police will simply assume I didn't want to face the repercussions of my supposed actions and took an early, accidental exit ramp.

Doris and Mark get away with everything.

That can't happen.

My daughter can't grow up with these people.

So I remain on the floor, eyes shut even though everything inside is screaming at me to open them again. There's a throbbing pain in my arm from where the needle broke off, but I don't so much as flinch. Mark needs to believe everything is still going to plan.

The front door opens and then slams shut. It's just Mark and me in the house now.

My ex-husband, the man I once loved. He just stabbed me in the arm with a needle so that he and his mother can kill me.

With my eyes shut, I don't know what's happening around me.

There hasn't been any movement, and it's making my heart pound. What is he doing?

I can hear him breathing from somewhere behind me, but don't dare open my eyes.

Finally I hear him step away, moving into the dining room for something. I want him to keep going, but he doesn't.

Sounds like he's opening a drawer in there or something, only steps away, which doesn't leave me any time to make a break for the front door.

There just isn't enough time. I'll only get one chance to use the element of surprise, so I have to time it right.

My eyes open, my pulse pounding. I'm facing away from Mark. My heart is beating so fast I'm almost afraid he's going to hear it tapping against the floorboards beneath me.

He's still in the other room. Should I jump up and try to make a run for it? Maybe I—

Squeaking shoes step close to my head as he comes back into the kitchen. The sound sends my heartbeat into the stratosphere.

Does he know I'm faking?

The silence stretches again, long enough that I'm desperate to open up my eyes. Anything could be happening around me, and I don't know what.

It's absolute havoc inside my mind, making staying still nearly impossible.

Then I feel his hands slide beneath my arms. He lets out a grunt as he hoists me upright. I fake a drunken murmur as if annoyed to be disturbed from my alcohol-induced slumber.

"I know, I know," Mark says with a grunt, "we'll get you home to bed, don't you worry."

As he picks me up, it takes everything I have not to fight him. Maybe I should, maybe this is my moment?

His head is right behind mine, and his focus is on hoisting me up from the floor. If I throw my head back with force, maybe it'll break his nose and give me a chance to get away.

Or maybe I'll miss him entirely and waste my one chance. Even if I do manage to make contact, he's much larger than me, and much more physical. I'm not sure a broken nose will do the trick.

Still, I need to do something before it's too late. Now that he's got me upright, I slouch against him, feigning barely being conscious. Mark throws an arm around my waist and lets out a snort of amusement as I slump.

It's utterly humiliating, and my entire body is on fire, but I don't react. I just allow myself to be picked up and carried through the house like a baby.

"Almost there," he says.

My arms dangle limply.

We enter the garage. There's Doris's car, a small black older-model sedan. It sits quietly, innocently. The same car she uses to drive my daughter to the playground, but for me it might as well be a hearse.

I know what'll happen if I allow myself to be placed into the backseat.

I've got to try something. I'm running out of time. If I don't, I'll never see my daughter again.

In the garage there are plenty of tools I could use to defend myself, but I'm in Mark's arms.

The second I start to move, he'll drop me to the ground, and then he'll be all over me. There's not enough time for me to grab a weapon. My throat is so tight I can hardly breathe as Mark reaches the car.

I'm expecting him to put me down to open the door—but he doesn't. Instead, he lets out a grunt and lifts a knee, balancing me between his body and the car while grabbing the back door handle with his left hand.

I hear it pop open, the noise sending a spear of panic through me. I'm out of time. I've got to fight back, right now.

I'm just about to leap into action when an idea explodes like a firework into my brain. A desperate, crazy idea.

It might be the only way I make it out of here alive.

As discreetly as I can, I crack open the eyelid on the right side of my face, which faces away from Mark.

I'm looking for something in the car. Please. Please be there.

When I see it, my entire body fills with adrenaline.

Mark doesn't seem to notice, as he's too busy shifting my weight again while trying to pry the car door open further with a knee.

Finally succeeding, he lays me down across the backseat, and I murmur again, but otherwise don't react.

Mark tucks my legs into the car then shuts the door. The second he does, I snap open my eye and reach toward Judith's prep pack which is tucked into the mesh pocket behind the driver's seat.

My wonderful, over-prepared sister.

I have only a couple seconds and can only use one arm. Otherwise, Mark will see the movement.

He pulls open his door just as I pull the small plastic box from the mesh. It lands on the carpeted floor of the car without noise as Mark lets out a cough and digs in his pocket for the car keys.

I can't see the box and feel around blindly for it. There—the tips of my fingers find the box and drag it closer. Placing my hand on top of it, I search for the latch that keeps it securely closed.

Without sight, I'm going by feel alone. Also my fingers are shaking.

When they finally manage to get the latch open, my entire system comes alive. A short, excited exhale of breath escapes my mouth, spiking my pulse as I hear Mark twist around in the seat.

I know he's looking at me. I remain completely still, fighting every instinct I have to move.

One second passes. Two. My whole body seems to pulse in time with my heartbeat.

Then I hear Mark turn back around, the leather seat squeaking as he pulls the driver's side door shut and jams the key into the ignition.

As the engine roars to life, I close my fingers around the small canister of pepper spray.

Judith, I love you.

My arms are hidden from Mark's view. My head is in the middle of the backseat, so my eyes stay closed in case he glances back at me again.

Keeping the rest of my body as still as possible, I carefully rotate the pepper spray in my hand until I'm holding it correctly.

Then I let out another murmur. As the leather seat squeaks again, letting me know Mark's turning to check on me, my eyelids snap open.

The world floods back into vision.

Our eyes meet—but only for a half-second, a single frame of calm before I press down on the pepper spray, and Mark begins to scream.

THIRTY-EIGHT
KATIE

The burn is unlike anything I've ever felt.

Even though the spray wasn't pointed at me, the fact we're in an enclosed space means I'm still feeling some of the effects. Tears stream from my eyes as I squint, my skin feeling like it's alight with flame.

Mark took a direct shot to the eyes, and his screaming makes my ears ring as I grope for the door handle.

I get my hands around it as the spray burns in my throat and lungs, making me cough raggedly. The door pops open, and I flop for the fresh air.

Mark lets out another scream, the seat rocking back and forth as he rubs at his eyes and thrashes around.

My body flops to the concrete as I crawl from the car, coughing and almost unable to open my eyes. When I hear Mark's door open though, I force an eyelid open despite the agony.

"Katie," Mark screams from behind me.

I hear him drop out of the car, but don't turn around. I'm staring at the wall, and the button for the garage door opener. Pushing back to my feet, I stumble toward it, my eyes opened only a few centimeters to take in the blur around me.

There's more grunting from behind me, though now it's less pain and more anger.

"Come here," he shouts, followed by a grunt of agony.

My hand smashes against the button, and the door comes to life to my left. Out of the corner of my eye, I see Mark pulling himself back to his feet as he rubs at his eyes with both hands.

"No," he shouts after me.

There's light—I can see light through the door opening that gets larger by the second. Freedom.

I scramble forward, eyes and body barely functional. Tears and mucus stream down my face as coughs wrack my body, but I fight forward.

Mark's right behind me. I can hear him coming.

Two more steps. Two more and I'm outside. The door is at waist-height, but I don't wait for it to go higher, diving underneath it instead.

I land hard on the rough asphalt of the driveway, my knees screaming with pain as my skin tears, but I don't stop, scrambling back up a second later to run for the street.

I'm screaming at the top of my lungs, and I can't tell whether it's the pepper spray or my terror-filled voice that tears my throat apart.

Mark's heavy footsteps behind me keep me going, pushing forward through the blur the world has become. I can just make out the outline of the fence and the gate. I push through it and spill out onto the street, still screaming.

If I can just—an iron grip clamps down on my wrist, nearly yanking my arm from its socket.

I whip around, coming face to face with Mark.

His eyes are barely open, so red and swollen it almost doesn't look like him. He's some red-faced monster that snarls at me as I try to pull away.

"Hey! What's going... Mark?"

Mark stops tugging against me as I look to our right, where a man stands on the sidewalk. He's staring at Mark with wide eyes. Further down the street there are more people who've come out of their houses to see what's going on.

My heart beats faster. I can see on Mark's face that he's realized his mistake. He's been seen alive.

It's over. It's all over.

His grip on my arm weakens, and I pull away, stumbling away from him as more people come out of their houses. I see people lifting phones to their ears to call the police, while others record.

"Mommy?"

I spin around, seeing Amelia running toward me. Behind her is an older woman and a small boy, both of them looking on in absolute confusion. I drop to my knees and hug Amelia, tears of joy, not pain, now streaming from my eyes.

My baby girl.

Mark's running back into Doris's house, still wiping at his eyes as he tries to hide. It's too late. He's been spotted, and that means the whole plan is going to fall apart.

I keep holding onto Amelia even as people come to check on me. Others shout for the police.

I drop down to the street as a sob wracks my body. A combination of adrenaline, despair, and utter relief that all of this is finally over.

Someone is squatting beside me, asking if I'm okay. I can't respond.

I just want to see my sister.

THIRTY-NINE

KATIE

Judith scowls at me.

"I hate you," she says.

"But fine. If that's what you want to watch, then that's what we're watching."

I grin at her. This is exactly the way I want to spend Thanksgiving, no need for a turkey or elaborate sides. Just a wonderful day spent surrounded by those I love. And bad movies.

Amelia rolls around between us on the couch.

"Is the popcorn done yet?" she asks.

I look at her, tucking a strand of her hair behind her head. "I don't know. I'll check."

"I'll join you," Judith says, hopping up with me.

We walk through the living room of her apartment to the kitchen. I've been staying here since Judith was released.

It's been a wild few days since the world realized Mark Wharton was still alive. What had been a case of only regional interest suddenly exploded onto national news.

This time, Judith and I talked to the media. Together.

The Rose sisters, reunited.

Mark was taken into custody shortly after our altercation in the street. The videos of him covered in pepper spray are still going viral. Doris was apprehended the following day.

Like mother, like son. Too bad they don't have Mommy and Me days in prison.

We've already been approached by two producers interested in developing our story for film. For now though, I just want to focus on spending time with those I care about. My family.

Judith and Amelia.

We step into the kitchen with the television still blaring from the other room as Amelia watches, entranced. It's been so wonderful having all of us together. Laughing, crying, growing closer.

Judith moves over to the microwave just as it dings to let us know the popcorn is ready. She pulls it out as I go for the spice rack, scooping up the cinnamon.

My sister sees me pick it up as she turns around. "Just like Mom used to make."

Suddenly she steps forward and pulls me into a hug.

"I love you so much," Judith says, squeezing me tight. "Thank you for not giving up on me."

"I love you too," I say back.

I mean it. I really, truly mean it. We are sisters, and that is a bond that can never be broken. The past few years have certainly tested it, that's for sure. But our bond is unbreakable, and I know that now.

"I'm just so thankful to have my little sister back," I say as we pull apart, giving Judith a wink.

Her eyes are wet as she lets out a chuckle. "Well, someone has to keep an eye on you."

We embrace again, holding tight. Despite all the craziness of the past few weeks, it's honestly been the best thing to ever happen to me.

I know now who I really am and exactly what I'm capable of—and what I'm not.

I have my daughter back. And I've got my built-in best-friend back.

When we separate, Judith steps over to the refrigerator and pulls it open.

"Can I get you anything to drink?" she asks.

"Water will be just fine," I say with a smile.

"Now, and for the rest of my life."

THANK you so much for reading *Which Sister*. I hope you enjoyed it. If you'd like to read my FREE psychological thriller novella, The Weekend Trip, sign up for my newsletter by heading to jackdanebooks.com. As a member of my mailing list, you'll be the first to know whenever I have a new book release and get behind the scenes information on my stories and my writing life.

If you had a great reading experience with this novel, would you mind taking a minute to post a review on

Amazon? A few words is all it takes, and it will truly make a difference in my career as an author.

Reviews are so important in helping other readers find great books that are worth their valuable time and attention.

Thanks so much for reading :)

Jack

ALSO BY JACK DANE

ABOUT THE AUTHOR

Jack Dane writes thrillers and psychological fiction that largely takes place in New York City, where he lives. When not writing, Jack enjoys going to jazz clubs, taking people-watching walks in the Park, and exploring the city by night, where he picks up ideas for his next book.

Get a FREE copy of his thriller novella *The Weekend Trip* by heading to jackdanebooks.com

You can connect with Jack on Facebook as well!

Printed in Dunstable, United Kingdom